"I think we should get married."

Darian tilted her head to one side. *I'm not hearing right*, she thought. "What?"

One corner of Tom's mouth rose. "I'm asking you to marry me."

She blinked. Twice. "What?"

"I know this seems sudden...but we know each other. We've become good friends. And we both want to be married, but we both have the same problem. We have no time to get to know someone, to court. I have a funny feeling about this. Like we were meant to meet. You know." He grinned. "Destiny."

That made her smile. He was quite a man. But what about Tom Steinbuck as a husband?

Her husband.

Dear Reader,

This month we have a terrific lineup of stories, guaranteed to warm you on these last chilly days of winter. March comes in like a lion with a great new FABULOUS FATHER by Donna Clayton. Joshua Kingston may have learned a thing or two about child-rearing from his son's new nanny, Cassie Simmons. But now the handsome professor wants to teach Cassie a few things about love! The *Nanny and the Professor* is sure to touch your heart.

Elizabeth August concludes her WHERE THE HEART IS series with *A Husband for Sarah*. You've watched Sarah Orman in previous titles bring couples together. Now Sarah gets a romance—and a wedding—all her own!

A *Wife Most Unlikely* is what Laney Fulbright is to her best friend, Jack Austin. But Laney's the only woman this sexy bachelor wants! Linda Varner brings MR. RIGHT, INC. to a heartwarming conclusion.

Alaina Hawthorne brings us two people who strike a marriage bargain in *My Dearly Beloved*. Vivian Leiber tells an emotional story of a police officer and the woman he longs to love and protect in *Safety of His Arms*. And this month's debut author, Dana Lindsey, brings us a handsome, lonely widower and the single mom who's out to win his heart in *Julie's Garden*.

In the coming months, look for books by favorite authors Suzanne Carey, Marie Ferrarella, Diana Palmer and many others.

Happy reading!

Anne Canadeo
Senior Editor
Silhouette Romance

Please address questions and book requests to:
Silhouette Reader Service
U.S.: 3010 Walden Ave., P.O. Box 1325, Buffalo, NY 14269
Canadian: P.O. Box 609, Fort Erie, Ont. L2A 5X3

MY DEARLY BELOVED

Alaina Hawthorne

Published by Silhouette Books
America's Publisher of Contemporary Romance

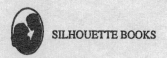

SILHOUETTE BOOKS

ISBN 0-373-19069-7

MY DEARLY BELOVED

Books by Alaina Hawthorne

Silhouette Romance

Out of the Blue #672
The Bridal Path #1029
My Dearly Beloved #1069

ALAINA HAWTHORNE,

a native Texan, has been writing fiction and non fiction since she was a teenager. Her first Silhouette Romance won the Romance Writers of America's RITA award for Best First Book. She lives in Houston with Sallie, her Rottweiler, and loves hearing from her readers.

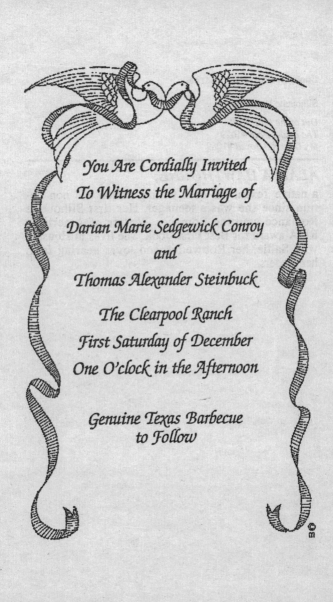

You Are Cordially Invited
To Witness the Marriage of
Darian Marie Sedgewick Conroy
and
Thomas Alexander Steinbuck

The Clearpool Ranch
First Saturday of December
One O'clock in the Afternoon

Genuine Texas Barbecue
to Follow

Chapter One

"The school called, Darian. Twice. They want you to come get Jason right away."

Darian Conroy stopped at her secretary's desk and set down her trial briefcase. "What?"

Marty Forteck shrugged slightly. "I told them you were in court until lunchtime. Dr. Bounds himself called the second time."

Darian squeezed her eyes closed for a moment. *Not again.* "Is Jason sick?" She knew her voice sounded hopeful, a fact she hated.

Marty didn't answer aloud but shook her head slowly. Her eyes reflected her concern and misgivings.

Darian sighed. "I didn't think so."

The phone rang again—a double ring. That meant an outside call.

"I'll get it in my office," Darian said. She took the messages off her spindle, shoved her office door open with her hip and grabbed the phone. "Darian Conroy," she said.

"Mrs. Conroy, this is Dr. Bounds." His voice was even more frosty and disapproving than the last time they'd spoken. "Did your secretary tell you that someone needs to come get Jason immediately?"

"Yes, Dr. Bounds, my secretary told me you called while I was in court. Is he—"

"Forgive me for interrupting, but something's going to have to be done about your son right away." The pitch of his voice began to rise, like a singer clawing for a note just out of reach. "Not only did he spend the morning freeing the rabbits that belong to Mrs. Weldon's first-graders, although you can imagine the mayhem that caused...."

Darian had seen Mrs. Weldon's first-graders so she wasn't particularly upset for the rabbits.

"... but before Mrs. Weldon could get him to my office, he ducked into the boys' rest room. For a cigarette."

A dull pain began to throb at Darian's temple. *What am I doing wrong?* "I see," she said quietly. "Are you sure?"

A momentary, glacial silence was Dr. Bounds's first reply. "Yes, Mrs. Conroy, I'm sure. And I must say, that although *in the past* Jason has been our most outstanding student, I have to consider the others here at Fullingham. And our standards. You know the atmosphere we maintain here. The highest learning. The highest ideals."

Not to mention the highest tuition in Austin, Texas. "I understand perfectly, Dr. Bounds. I'll be there in twenty minutes."

When he hung up, Darian listened to the accusatory buzz of the dial tone. A faint needling pain spiraled slowly up her shoulders to her nape and joined the throb at her temples. What's gone wrong? she wondered. Jason had always been such a good kid. So caring. So responsible for a ten-year-old.

Joel Conroy's face flashed through her mind, and she felt her jaw tighten. He hadn't phoned his son in years. Darian couldn't even remember the last time they'd seen Joel. She wondered if he'd lost his hair or gotten fat. She hoped so, although she knew better. Her ex-husband had always been slim, and his shaggy, thick hair probably still fell with boyish charm over his wide, intelligent forehead and into his huge, sincere-looking eyes.

Don't just sit there blaming somebody else. You've got things to do and this isn't helping. She jumped out of her chair and tugged down her suit jacket. Jason was her responsibility and hers alone. She'd accepted that years ago when she was struggling through law school with a baby and an absentee husband. She had been so young then. So in love. So stupid.

She punched out Richard Acker's extension and asked him to take her two-o'clock appointment, then grabbed her purse. *Jason smoking?* It seemed so unlikely, considering the way he complained about smoke if they were in a restaurant. She'd get to the bottom of this at the school, then bring her son back to the office. After that she'd finish her afternoon's work and take him to dinner. They could have a long heart-to-heart talk and maybe she could find out what was going on. But then, of course, she'd have to come back to the office. She and Richard would have to work all weekend revising the discovery answers that had to be filed on Monday.

The case wasn't huge, but the partnership committee
was now watching every move the trial associates made.
Working all weekend was common for associates at the
firm, especially since this was Darian's seventh year—the
year she would make partner. Or not.

At least Jason was scheduled to go on a school field
trip that weekend. Darian needed to spend at least fifteen hours at the office both Saturday and Sunday.
They'd already booked the word-processing time. As
soon as the thought crossed her mind, she pressed her lips
together and squeezed her eyes closed. There was no way
Jason would be allowed to participate in the trip. And
there was no one at home to watch him because she'd
given Mrs. Steen the weekend off. Finding a sitter on
Friday afternoon would be impossible.

"Well, son of mine," she said aloud, "it looks like
you'll be camping out in the associates' lounge." He'd be
sullen and bored. Too bad, she thought. He could be
spending the weekend at Astroworld and the museum.

She punched the call button for an elevator, and in
moments the polished brass doors slid open.

"Ah, Darian, just who I wanted to see."

Atwell Huntingdon, the senior administrative partner, stepped out of the elevator. Two associates carrying
briefcases and file boxes slipped out behind him and
scuttled away, while he paused and leveled his cold gaze
straight into Darian's eyes. He looked satisfied, she
thought. Like a well-fed shark. Obviously things were
going well with the Burton Oil trial.

Darian smiled. "Well, then I'm glad I ran into you,
too, Atwell. What can I do for you?"

He tipped his head to the side and gave her another
deep, assessing look. His angular, handsome face was
unsoftened by either warmth or humor. The associates

called him Attila Huntingdon. "Do you have a minute? You look like you're on your way somewhere."

Darian felt a slight clutch in her middle. She hated what she had to say next. "I was just on the way to my son's school. He needs a ride home now."

She saw his reaction, subtle but unmistakable. The tiniest twitch of irritation. Of disapproval. She knew he was thinking there should be someone else to handle this sort of thing. Personal concerns should never interfere with firm business. And they should never, *ever* encroach on the firm's time. He, of course, had a wife at home to take care of his children.

"Nothing serious I hope," he said in an oily voice.

"No, not really. Just a mix-up in communication, I think." Darian kept her smile plastered firmly on her face.

Atwell made a sympathetic noise, but there was no compassion in his slate-colored eyes. "Good, good," he murmured. "I wanted to speak with you about representing the firm at a charity function—a silent auction and barbecue at Tom Steinbuck's ranch up in Wimberley. I was going to attend personally, but I'm in trial right now."

I'm not exactly waiting for the second coat of polish to dry myself. Darian forced her smile to broaden. Atwell Huntingdon sat on the partnership committee, and despite the inconvenience of one more duty, there was no doubt he was handing her a plum of a task. The Steinbucks were Texas aristocracy, political heavyweights and big names in the oil field, as well. Besides being a test, this kind of assignment was also small reward. Now that Darian had proved herself to be a capable attorney, her social savvy was being tested.

"I'd be honored to represent the firm, Atwell. Thank you for thinking of me."

"We have the highest confidence in you, Darian, but may I suggest that you take another associate along? Perhaps Richard Acker."

Darian nodded thoughtfully. "That'll work out well. Richard and I are already working together, so our schedules will be easy to coordinate."

"Fine, fine. Well, I don't want to hold you up. We can talk about it when you get back this afternoon." He blinked coldly. "You are planning to come back, aren't you?"

Darian concentrated on keeping her expression pleased and calm. "Of course. What time would you like to meet?"

"Let's say two-thirty."

"Good. I'll see you then." Perspiration slickened her palms, and the tingling pain at the base of her neck turned fiery. She'd have to put the pedal to the metal to make it to the school and back in time. Just as she turned to punch for another elevator she heard his voice again.

"Oh, Darian," Atwell said.

She turned in time to see once again his glittering, humorless smile.

"Yes."

"This function. It's tomorrow."

She swallowed. "Wonderful," she said. "I'm looking forward to it."

He nodded, then turned and walked toward his office, his Italian loafers silent on the plush, neutral-colored carpet.

Darian's heart sank. Wimberley was almost an hour outside Austin. Let's see, she thought. An hour there, another back. At least two or three hours at this stupid dog-and-pony show. "Damn," she muttered. "We'll lose most of the day." That meant working all night. Again. Probably Sunday night, too. The elevator doors closed behind her with a quiet thump, and she let her shoulders sag.

This wasn't the first time the demands of her life had seemed overwhelming. In fact, the closer she came to achieving her goals, the more grueling her schedule seemed.

And now this business with Jason.

Am I being a bad mother? she wondered. Is my work causing me to neglect him? No, she thought. As a single mother with no other support, she'd have to work hard under the best of circumstances. Besides, the time she put in at the firm was what enabled Jason to go to a school that could challenge him and develop his intellect and talents. They lived in a beautiful home in a safe neighborhood. They took nice vacations together. Besides, Darian wanted to inspire her son with her own example; to show him she had a complete life outside motherhood.

And every bit as important to Darian was her commitment to herself, her own talents and abilities. She had a duty to fulfill her own potential. After all, Jason was growing up, and someday soon he'd be out on his own. She owed her best to herself, to her firm and to her clients. She had obligations to her community and a special commitment to volunteer work for deserted women and children. She would make partner; she would live up to her potential and still be a good mother.

She would show her son that a person could achieve professional success without having to sacrifice family. She would prove that Joel was wrong—you don't have to desert your family in order to be successful.

So far she thought she'd lived up to all her commitments, and she'd still done everything any woman could do to be a good mother. A year ago she'd even started leaving work in the afternoon in order to be home when Jason got back from school; then, after nine, she would return to the office and work into the small hours of the morning. Mrs. Steen lived in, so Jason was never alone. So why, in the most important year of her career, the year she was eligible to make partner, why had her son decided to have a personality crisis?

With a sigh, Darian threw her purse in her car, pulled onto Congress Street and into the noontime traffic.

Twenty minutes later she parked her car and ran up the shallow steps to the Fullingham Academy. Inside, the quiet building smelled of floor wax, old wallpaper and disinfectant. Darian walked briskly, and the click of her heels echoed as she walked down the hall to the principal's office. This was the fourth time she'd made that walk this year, and they weren't even through October yet.

Julia, the receptionist, smiled as Darian approached her desk. She was a comfortable-looking, middle-aged woman with thick glasses perched on her thin nose. "I'll tell him you're here," she whispered. Julia always whispered and Darian never knew why.

When Darian turned around she saw Jason sitting in the chair by the door. He was swinging his legs slightly and gazing at her with huge, tragic eyes. At that moment they looked exactly like Joel's. He gave Darian a tentative smile and lifted his hand. "Hi, Mom."

Darian let her own gaze narrow. "Hello, Jason. I suppose you know I'm not very pleased to be here."

"I figured," he said simply and pushed his hair away from his eyes. His hair was like hers—thick, dishwater blond and straight as string. "I'm sorry you had to come. Are they mad at you at the office?"

"I really don't care to discuss my job with you right now, Jason. Besides, if you were really concerned about my career, I don't think you'd be pulling stunts like you did today. I hear you were smoking. Did you enjoy it? You'll be lucky if they don't expel you. Now I have to go charm Dr. Bounds into letting you stay."

His gaze fell to his lap and he began picking at his fingernails. Darian heard a door open behind her. "Mrs. Conroy."

She turned. "Dr. Bounds," she said walking forward, hand extended. "I'm sorry to have taken longer to get here than I said, but Atwell Huntingdon caught me on the way out of the office. You know Mr. Huntingdon, don't you? Both of his sons graduated from Fullingham."

Dr. Bounds blinked and seemed slightly flustered. He had the wary, disapproving look of a man who knows he's being bamboozled but can't quite figure out how. He narrowed his eyes and puckered suspiciously. "Oh, of course. How is Atwell?"

"Oh, just fine." Darian swept past Dr. Bounds and into his office. "He sends his best. Shall I sit here? Thank you. Now, what happened this morning?"

Thirty minutes later Darian stood outside Dr. Bounds's door and shook his hand again. "Thank you so much for being so understanding. My mother has always said Fullingham is the only school in Austin, probably in Texas, that really challenges exceptional children. I think the counseling you've suggested is just what Jason needs. You know, I have to agree it's really difficult for him sometimes without a strong male figure in his life."

"I'm glad we understand each other, Mrs. Conroy. I hope I don't have to make another call like today's."

"I hope so, too. Thank you, again."

Darian turned to face Jason whose feet swung slowly to a stop. She saw his eyes widen and almost heard the strangled gulp as he swallowed. "Come along, Jason. You and I have some talking to do."

The next morning Darian sat in the passenger seat of Richard Acker's four-wheel drive and tried to read case law while he jounced along the blacktop two-lane through Dripping Springs.

"Are we there yet, Richard?" Jason's voice rose peevishly from the back seat.

"That's Mr. Acker to you, Jason," Darian said, as she pushed her reading glasses back up her nose. They'd been in the car less than half an hour, and Jason had started complaining almost immediately. She knew he was tired, cranky and very disappointed about missing the trip to Houston.

"About twenty minutes more, dude," Richard said cheerfully.

Richard's jaunty voice grated slightly on Darian's nerves. Richard was always cheerful. He was single, thirty and didn't have any kids. Or any gray hair, Darian noted. She turned away from *Morton On Contracts* and chewed the end of her yellow highlighter as she looked out the window.

The Texas hill country rolled by, a rugged, tough landscape of juniper, black oaks and cedar. Darian had hardly looked up during the drive and so she didn't see the change from Austin's rolling hills and little jeweled lakes to the hill country's rocky shoulders, sudden canyons and shallow creeks, shaggy with overhanging cypress.

"I think we're there, guys," Richard said. "Yep. Clearpool Creek Road."

Clearpool Ranch would have been easy to find that day even without the weather-beaten sign. A column of luxury sedans and limousines threaded their way in a sluggish line down the narrow county road and over a cattle guard. When Richard's tires clattered over the pipe barrier, Darian abandoned her study of the intricacies of *Brookwood versus Timley.*

After five more minutes down the twisting, unpaved ranch road, a brown uniformed state trooper directed them to join a parallel line of parked vehicles. Darian's eyebrows raised. Car after car bore the exempt plates of federal judges, state judges and United States senators. She sat up and wondered briefly if her long denim skirt and chambray shirt were suitable. A quick look around reassured her. This was Texas chic. Everyone would be wearing denims. The only way to tell who was who would be by the name tags. Or the jewelry.

As soon as the engine grumbled into silence, Jason's sullen voice again rose from the backseat. "How long do we have to stay?"

Darian turned and fixed her son with a cold glare. "Jason McGreevy Conroy, listen to me good. I told you last night how important this is. And I also told you there would be ponies to ride and plenty of food and hayrides and other stuff to entertain kids. And one more thing, young man." She took his knee firmly in her hand. "You're lucky you're not spending the weekend in your room. If you do one thing to embarrass me or get into trouble, not only will you lose your allowance for six more weeks, there won't be any trips with the school for six months. Do you understand me?"

Jason's color rose and his eyes, so like his father's, grew huge and shiny. "Yes, ma'am."

"Good. Now follow me and we'll find the ponies." Darian felt a nauseating grip under her sternum. She detested arguing with her son. Lately, though, it was all they seemed to do.

She turned toward Richard and rolled her eyes. He grinned in a maddeningly jovial way. "Let's try to leave here by three, Dee. Is that okay with you?"

"Three sounds good," she said. "It's noon right now and they're supposed to tally the bids at two-thirty. Where do you think the auction is?"

Richard turned in a slow circle. "Can't be in the house. There. There's a tent behind the barn."

Darian turned and squinted. Just peeking around the corner of a red picture-postcard barn, she could see the striped blue-and-white canvas of a circus-size tent. She took a deep breath, and for the first time she noticed how sweet the air was. October smelled different here—clean and sharp with pine. And it was cooler here than in Austin. "Yeah, I see it. Let's go." She turned and looked down at her son who was actually beginning to gaze around with interest. "Come on, honey, this could be fun."

He immediately dropped his head and grumbled something about being hungry. Darian sighed and turned to follow Richard toward the tent. As the three of them walked across the freshly mowed field, Darian recognized some of the other guests milling in knots under the shade trees and leaning against the high, whitewashed planks of the fence. Strange, she thought, to see them outside of the courtroom—out of their fiercely correct suits and power ties. Smiling at one another. Being charming. She remembered the World War II story about the German and British soldiers laying aside their weapons to play soccer with each other on Christmas Day.

To their left rose a mellow-colored two-story ranch house of native stone with deep windows and an angular, soaring roof. The porch was wide and flagstone-paved, and the pillars holding up the second-story porch were all shaggy rough-hewn cedar. Pots of fall flowers squatted cheerfully by comfortable-looking rawhide furniture, and antique harness and implements were hammered to the walls.

"Pretty house," Darian murmured. "It's bigger than I thought it'd be."

"Yeah," Richard said. "Steinbucks have been around a long time and they were always loaded. Cattle money, oil money, railroad. Real estate all over Texas. Besides the political connections."

"Tuffy Steinbuck's been dead for years, hasn't he?" Darian asked. She knew the old man was called the King Maker because of his influence in Texas politics during the forties and fifties.

"About eight or ten or so, I think," Richard said. "My father used to come hunting here. So you've never been to one of these things, huh?"

"Uh-uh," Darian replied, craning her neck to look over the crowd. "My family's from Dallas. Education, not politics."

A band was playing somewhere inside the tent, and Darian heard the happy sawing of a fiddle and the chest-rattling thud of a bass guitar turned up high. She smiled. She hadn't known there would be live music.

Just as they were approaching the tent, she saw a group of people standing by the raised tent flaps. Her eyes widened slightly as she recognized two name partners from a high-powered plaintiffs' firm talking to an astonishing redhead whom she was certain she'd seen modeling lingerie in *Chemise*. But most striking of all was one tall, broad-shouldered, tanned man.

He wore jeans, but not in the self-conscious, cowboy-for-a-day manner of those around him. His clothes had been washed and disciplined into intimate familiarity with every muscle and sinewy curve of his hips and long legs. The arms crossed over his broad chest were long and muscular, and he stood with his back arched, rocking slightly on his heels. His boots were exotics—the kind that must have cost thousands when they were new—just like his jacket, and although his brown Stetson shadowed his face, it didn't obscure the brilliance of his smile, or soften the rough angles of his jaw or cheekbones.

Darian frowned slightly. He certainly wasn't classically handsome, but definitely compelling. Charismatic even at a distance. She felt herself wanting to stare. "Who's that?"

Richard glanced over, then back. "That's our host, Tom Steinbuck."

"Tall, isn't he?"

Richard gave her a knowing look. "Is this a note of interest I detect, counselor?"

Darian huffed slightly and rolled her eyes. "Oh, for heaven's sake, Richard. All I said was I think the guy is tall."

He gave her a look of mock injury. "You never thought I was tall."

"Let's go find the barbecue," she said dryly.

When they passed close to the group, Darian felt a prickling sensation along her nape. Something besides peripheral vision told her that Tom Steinbuck had seen her and noticed her, too. She took a quick breath and shook the feeling off. "Don't be dumb, Darian," she muttered. "You've already got more to do than you can handle."

The interior of the tent droned with the low thunder of several hundred people talking at once. Adding to the pleasant rumble was the distant clatter of catering and an occasional explosion of laughter. All around them people stood, talking, drinking and eating red spicy-looking food from plates much too small for the ribs and potato salad piled on them.

On the opposite side of the tent a heavy velvet rope swagged between stainless-steel poles to separate the items donated for auction. Darian could see paintings, a statue or two and several glass cases that she assumed covered jewelry. "Are you guys starving, or do you want to look around?"

"Starving," Richard replied as his gaze swept the crowd, alight with the predatory gleam of a born politician. "That's Carla Freeman over there. I'll need to schmooze soon."

"You barracuda. Feel free to schmooze away. I'm going to go start our bidding."

"By the way, what are we supposed to buy?"

Darian breathed importantly. "Well, I have six thousand to buy a set of fifteen antique Lone Star flags from the Republic era." She held up the program and read, "Item number twenty-two. Bidding to start at three thousand, please."

"Just what the firm needs," Richard said. "More junk in the partners' lounge."

"Show a little reverence, Acker," Darian replied, with mild disgust. "This is for charity."

Suddenly, just at her left elbow, Jason went rigid with excitement. "Oh, cool. Look, Mom." For one instant he dragged at her sleeve and pointed toward the auction line. "A Hummie." Then he lunged away like a dolphin arching through water and disappeared behind a small group to her left.

Darian whirled around and whipped her gaze back and forth. "What? Where? Jason, wait." She shouldered her way through the closeness of the crowd in time to see her son slide under the rope barrier, and rest both hands on the cherry-red chassis of a squat little vehicle. The stainless-steel grille and bulbous headlights gave it the look of a giant, cheerful, alien frog. Jason threw a glance over his shoulder. "It's a Hummie, Mom. Isn't it cool? Do you think I can ride it?" His voice trailed away to an ardent and awestruck murmur. "A Hummie."

Darian knew she looked bewildered. She was. "A what?"

"Excuse me, ma'am, but that's a seventy-five-horsepower all-terrain automatic low-noise Hummerfeldt Landskimmer."

The deep voice hit Darian just at the nape of her neck, and countless unseen fibers along her spine sprang to sudden attention like metal shavings suddenly attracted by powerful magnetism. She turned to face the owner of the baritone. She had known it would be him.

He touched the brim of his hat. "Like the fella says, a Hummie." He extended his hand. "Tom Steinbuck."

"Darian Conroy," she replied, accepting his handshake. He took her hand like he would a man's, strong and firm. Darian liked that. "So this is your home. I envy you getting to live in the hill country."

Something indefinable flickered through his blue eyes. "Yes, ma'am. I'm a lucky man." He looked down at Jason and smiled. "So, d'you ride ATVs, son?"

The boy's eyes pleaded. "Oh, yeah. I'm sure I could."

"Jason Conroy," Darian's said reproachfully. "You've never been on one of those things in your life." She smiled up at their host. "This is my son, Jason. Jason, this is Mr. Steinbuck."

Jason stood. "I'm pleased to meet you, Mr. Steinbuck," he said, and solemnly took the tall rancher's hand. Then his bright face turned tragic and urgent. "Can I go for a ride?"

Tom Steinbuck's face screwed into a wary expression, and he crossed his arms and stood just the way Darian had seen him stand earlier. "Well, Jason, I'm not sure. I donated it for the auction and there's already some bids on it, so it's not mine to say anymore, but later on I just might be—"

Tom's voice was interrupted by a canine yelp of such longing and despair that all three of them turned simultaneously to face the area just on the other side of the little buggy. A spotted puppy eyed them for a moment, and seeing herself noticed, flung her body desperately against the wire of her travel cage.

A soft noise somewhere between a moan and a sigh fell from Jason's mouth, and he abandoned the Hummie. He didn't even look back at Darian, but threw himself on his knees at the cage and poked his fingers through the wire to be enveloped by a frantic pink tongue.

Darian stifled her smile and glanced up at the man standing next to her. "Well, Mr. Steinbuck, so much for the Hummie," she said. He looked down and gave her a conspiratorial wink.

Although Darian was five-nine in her bare feet—nearly two inches taller in her bottle-green, designer cowboy boots—she had to tip her head back to look into Tom Steinbuck's indigo eyes.

"'The fleeting affections of callow youth,'" he quoted with a twinkle. "Please call me Tom." The way he spoke, his request didn't seem at all like casual small talk; it was more like a favor, asked with respect.

Darian smiled, feeling oddly complimented. "Well, thank you. But only if you'll call me Darian."

"I thought you'd never ask." This time when he smiled, she could see the deep creases the sun had made at the corners of his eyes. Thirty-five, she thought. Maybe even forty.

"Mom, c'm'ere."

She sighed. "Oh, what now?"

Jason's face glowed. "Isn't she beautiful, Mom? The cardboard auction thingie says she's a German short-hair. Isn't she great?"

Before Darian could answer, a florid, red-faced man moved through the crowd toward them. He stopped just outside the rope barrier—his saucer-size belt buckle nearly obscured by his enormous belly and his pants riding dangerously low on his hips. Gravity had dragged his loose jowls down over his collar, and Darian knew it was just a matter of time before the g forces took hold of his pants, too.

"Git away from thar, boy," he said. He gestured at Jason with a picked-clean rib bone clutched in fingers greasy with barbecue sauce. "That ain't no play toy."

Jason gave him a stony look and turned back to the dog. "Can't I just take her out to play? She really wants to play with me."

As soon as the huge man noticed Darian's companion, he tipped his head in a respectful nod. "Tom," he said. Even though he'd swallowed the mouthful of meat, his voice still sounded thick and full of food. "That there's Winfield's Princess of Warwick. Me and Maude donated her and two years training with Ed Sigafoos at Round Top. You know Sigafoos, don'tcha, Tom?" He nodded at Darian. "Zat your boy, ma'am? Tell 'im she ain't that kind of dog. She's a hunting dog. Field-trial dog. If she turns out to be a good 'un, she'll be a momma dog."

"Jason, come away," Darian said firmly. "The puppy belongs to this man."

The boy looked up at Darian, eyes glowing. Love-struck. "She wants out, Mom. She wants to play with me."

Tom stepped forward. "Luther, this is Darian Conroy and her son, Jason. Darian, this is Luther Winfield."

The huge man extended a shiny hand, and Darian struggled to repress her recoil reflex. Then she saw he was merely extending to her his business card. "Winfield Oil, ma'am. Who're you with?"

"Uh, I, Sternwell and Haig. In Austin."

From the corner of her eye, she could see the information register with Tom Steinbuck. She could tell by the slight deepening of his smile creases that the news somehow pleased him or confirmed something that he'd known or suspected.

"Well, Miss Conroy, tell your boy we don't play with hunting dogs. Roughhousing with her'll just give her bad habits. Make her beg, y'know. Spoil her."

"Come away, Jason," Darian said, softly. "Sorry, Mr. Winfield. Little boys just naturally love puppies, I guess."

His grunted reply was lost on Jason who stood up, red-faced, lips trembling. "Can we go home? I want to go home."

Instantly Darian wanted to throttle him. Why did he have to act this way? What was going wrong with her son?

"You don't want to leave now, Jason," Tom said, quietly, his deep voice somehow soothing despite the slightest tinge of reproach. "They're saddling up ponies behind the barn right now."

Jason's gaze snapped to his mother's face. "Can I go, Mom?"

She glanced tiredly at her watch. "Sure, honey. Do you want me to go with you?"

"C'mon, mom, I'm not a little kid. I can go by myself."

"Well, okay," she said reluctantly. "But meet me back here at two-thirty, okay?"

He nodded at her, ignored Tom and gave Luther Winfield a glare of pure disgust.

Winfield disappeared back into the crowd, and Darian found herself alone with her host. "My son isn't usually such a pill," she said softly. "He's having a hard time right now."

Tom Steinbuck stood in front of her, kind-eyed and rock-solid. He crossed his arms and took his chin thoughtfully. "I liked him. He likes dogs and he recognizes a good engine. He'll make a good man."

Even though he was obviously being conciliatory, his compassion warmed her. "I don't know if you really mean that, but it sure was the right thing to say."

"Of course I meant it," Tom said. He looked around, seeming suddenly at a loss, or irritated at the crowd surging around them. "Would you like a glass of wine?

Or some barbecue? It's Durango Company. Hill country's hottest."

Darian gave a little sigh and smiled. How long had it been since she'd had a meal with a man without eating it across a negotiating table? Eight years? Nine? She suddenly realized that the customary knot between her shoulders had unraveled and had been replaced by an easy warmth. "Tempting," she said with a smile, "but I'm not really very hungry, and I think I'd better turn in my bid."

"Well, okay, but after that, since I can't ply you with food or wine, how'd you like to tour the Steinbuck Old Place? It's a little quieter than this. The house is in the National Register."

Suddenly the shrieks and laughter of the other guests seemed tinged with hysteria. "I'd love to," she said, and glanced up and down the long rows of goods on display. "Do you know where the Lone Star flags are?"

"This way, ma'am." He turned sideways and offered her his elbow. She took it. There were two other unenthusiastic bids for the flags, so Darian filled out the card and, feeling freer than she had in weeks, she followed Tom out into the crisp October air.

"I hope I'm not dragging you away from your guests," Darian said.

"Not at all," he said. "I've enjoyed about as much of this as I can stand for one day."

In the moment he looked down at her, Darian sensed a kindred spirit—someone as tired as she was of a grueling life and happy to find a pleasant island of time with an attractive, interesting stranger. She smiled up at him, not offended in the least by his bluntness.

There were a few other people in the old stone house, all obviously friends or employees of Tom's. He introduced Darian and then she lost track of time as they wandered through the old stone and rough-hewn rooms. The house was filled with good art, photographs and memorabilia from the past eighty years—huge deer hunts and dove hunts. Dances, roundups and weddings.

It had the snug, pleasant smell of furniture polish and nice food. The walls were lined with books, Indian rugs and collections in glass cases, photographs and the aged, shabby trophies of hunts from time out of mind. There was also the quiet magic of an odd little museum and the sleepy, inviting comfort of a lived in home. It was the kind of place where you knew, if you wanted, you could find a quiet room, curl up with one of the old books and go to sleep and no one would mind.

On an ancient upright piano, Darian noticed a picture of Tom and a very old man wearing a battered straw cowboy hat, standing alongside a stunning middle-aged woman. Her smile was wide and brilliant, and she had the most devilishly wicked eyes Darian had ever seen.

"Are these your folks?" Darian asked.

"Yes, that's Tuffy and Daphne. Mom lives in Corpus now." His voice sounded a little regretful, but not truly sad.

"You miss her?"

"Oh, I don't let her stay gone long enough to miss her." He paused and straightened the photograph. "I do miss him, though. The older I get, the more things I wish I would have asked him."

Darian thought of her father. "I know what you mean." Her gaze fell to her wristwatch. "Good grief, it's after two."

Tom frowned. "Damn. I guess we'd better get back. I'm the official bid announcer."

"Thanks for sharing your house with me. It's amazing."

He looked down at her. "Thanks for being amazed by my old house."

As they walked back toward the tent, Darian could hardly believe she'd spent so much time just wandering around the house and talking with Tom. She hadn't laughed so easily or felt so relaxed in years. Then she realized it was probably because she put him at ease, too. Instinct told her he was a private man with plenty of his own pressures. She felt a twist of regret. She'd probably never see him again. Just as well, she thought. No time for that kind of thing.

The sun was angling toward the rugged hills, and spokes of golden and vermilion light pierced a thunderhead boiling high in the sky above them. The crisp fall air felt cool in Darian's lungs as she breathed deeply again. Tom seemed lost in his own thoughts.

As soon as they stepped into the tent, Darian could see that something had gone wrong. Two khaki-uniformed state troopers stood talking to Luther Winfield. He gestured angrily down and to his left. As they drew closer, Darian saw what had him so upset. The wire door of the puppy's cage had been pulled open. Next to the empty cage was an equally empty square of bright green artificial turf. The void where the little all-terrain vehicle had been parked seemed particularly conspicuous, like the gap left by a missing front tooth.

"There you are, Tom," Luther said, when he looked their way. "You need to call Joe Bob in. Someone's taken the Princess and that—that motorcycle thing, too."

Darian dropped back and let Tom join the other men. His face showed concern, but he didn't seem nearly as angry as Luther. Little groups of people, all with eyebrows raised, glanced their way. Darian noticed that none of the other more-expensive auction items seemed to be missing, and she wondered who, in company like this, would dream of making off with property donated for charity. What struck her as even more odd was that both items were relatively large and neither was terribly expensive. At least not compared to the artifacts and jewelry the thief could have stolen. She backed slowly away, intending to melt into the crowd, arrange for the delivery of the flags and head back to Austin.

Across the tent, she saw Richard excuse himself and thread his way through the crowd toward her. When he passed close to Luther, Tom and the officers, he raised his eyebrows at what was obviously an unfolding scandal.

Darian frowned as she again stared at the empty puppy cage, and then at the little platform where the Hummie had been parked. At that moment, somewhere deep within her, she heard a kind of distant, warning clang.

Richard stopped next to her, eyeing with detached curiosity the escalating activity surrounding the missing property. "We'd better head out soon if we're going to get anything done tonight." He glanced again toward the knot of men gathering around the empty dog cage. "By the way," he said. "Where's Jason?"

Chapter Two

"Tom, may I speak with you, please?"

When he turned to look down at her, Darian could see his blue eyes had gone dark and flat with concern. The other men gathered around him didn't try to hide their impatience. "Excuse me for a minute, Luther. Joe Bob."

Darian backed up several steps, crossed her arms and looked up at him. "I believe I know what happened to the ATV. And the puppy."

Tom's expression never changed. "Jason?"

Darian nodded.

"I was afraid so," he said quietly. "When I saw the way he looked at that dog, I knew he meant to have her out of her cage." There was a note of amusement, almost admiration, in his tone, although something in his look apologized for it. He didn't seem at all angry. "I've put the word out, and some of the men here are starting a search. I want to do this without embarrassing anybody."

"Thanks, Tom. I appreciate that." Darian's heart was pounding, and there was a bad taste in her mouth. Besides worrying about Jason, she felt humiliated by the inconvenience to Tom and his guests. Not to mention what the partners would say once they found out about the stunt her son had pulled. "I can't figure out how he could have started the engine. He's never been on one of those things."

Tom rubbed the suntanned skin under his eyes and then nudged his hat back with a callused knuckle. "You'd be surprised how easy they are to operate. Has he ever driven a go-cart?"

Her expression was his answer.

He shrugged. "There you go."

Darian felt more miserable and angry by the minute. *How could you be so irresponsible? This would never have happened if you hadn't wandered off to entertain yourself with your host. What kind of mother are you, anyway?* She swallowed hard. "I'm really sorry about this. Who's looking for them? I think I should go along."

"Now don't get upset, and don't go blaming yourself," Tom said. "I'm sure they'll show up in a little while. This wouldn't be the first time a good kid went for a joyride."

Before Darian could answer him, Luther Winfield set up a bellow about the ruination of his dog and the generally degenerate state of small boys. Darian grimaced. Obviously he'd come to the same conclusion she and Tom had. Tom followed her gaze, and he turned back and gave her a knowing and reassuring smile. "Don't worry about that old warthog. I'll go take care of Luther and then we'll go find your son."

Darian nodded and tried to smile back, but she knew it was pointless; her feelings were bound to show in her expression. This wasn't courtroom poker, this was her son whom she was obviously failing miserably in some fundamental way. "Thanks. I'll wait here."

When he turned and walked away, Darian tightened her grip on her upper arms. Although she was more angry than worried about Jason, she wanted him back *now*. The sun was barely sliding to the west, and she was surrounded by responsible, mature men and women, so if worse came to worst there were plenty of people to help her find him. And besides that, she couldn't stand to just wait around; she wanted to take action immediately—to march out across the pastures, find Jason and drag him back by his ear.

Then arrange to have him marooned on a desert island.

Soon after Tom walked away, Richard joined her. "You were right, Dee. The guy with the ponies said Jason rode for a while, but he left about an hour ago. I guess he sprang the puppy and then took off. One of the cooks says he's pretty sure he saw them going through the pasture behind the barn."

"Thanks, Richard. I'll tell Tom as soon as he's through."

"Come on, counselor," he said, his relentless jauntiness maddeningly in place. "Don't worry. It's just a typical kid thing. I bet we find him in less than an hour."

"I know he'll be okay, Richard. But I just want him back right now."

Richard stole a guilty look at his watch. "Well, actually, he did choose a pretty lousy day to pull something like this."

Darian could see that he didn't want to be insensitive, but Richard had his own pressures. In fact they should both be headed back to Austin now. They had interrogatories to revise for a Monday filing. Saturday secretaries and word processors would be waiting for them at the firm. She took a deep breath and turned to see how Tom was doing with Luther.

Winfield wore the dug-in, belligerent look of an angry toad, and although Darian hardly knew Tom, she could see he was beginning to lose his temper. Winfield continued to shout and gesticulate, his heavy jowls quivering and flapping. Some of the other guests were beginning to stare and murmur.

Finally, with a look of utter disgust, Tom turned and walked back. As he walked up, he gave Richard a quick nod. "Hello, Acker," he said quietly, and shook Richard's hand. "Good to see you again. Darian, I'm sorry, but Luther says he's leaving now and he wants a receipt for his dog. He's threatening all kinds of stupid business, and I know most of it's hot air, but he's talking about calling your firm."

Richard cursed softly. Darian squeezed her eyes shut.

"How much for the puppy?"

"Even though no one's bid for the dog, he swears she's worth at least eight hundred. If she's not back on time he'll lose his deduction."

Richard cursed again—this time with gusto. "Eight hundred dollars for a *dog?*"

Tight-lipped and seething, Darian reached in her purse and wrote the check and held it out to Tom. "Would you mind taking care of this for me. I'm afraid if I say one word to that—"

"I'll do it," said Richard. "I'm good at this." He took the check and walked away.

Darian looked back at Tom. "Now, what about the, uh, the—"

"The Hummie?" Tom tilted his head to the side. "I don't see any problem at all there as long as we get it back. Dave Alexander is in with the high bid, and he's a good friend of mine. He's got three boys of his own so he'll probably be understanding. I've sent a couple of people to look for him." He turned and glanced over his shoulder. "I have to go announce the high bids, but I'll be back as soon as I can. Wait, here's Dave."

Tom introduced them, then pulled the other man aside for a moment. As soon as they finished speaking, Dave turned, nodded to Darian and left quickly. "He's gone to send his sons home for some horses. The boys will ride the fence line."

"Oh, thank you. I want to do something to help, but I don't quite know—"

He glanced down at her, and his eyes were warm and reassuring. "You can help by not worrying so much. Everything's going to be okay."

Darian nodded unenthusiastically. Despite Tom's kindness, she felt worse with every passing moment. After all, this was an important social function. What would he think of her? Of Jason? What would Atwell Huntingdon say when he found out? There would be all sorts of embarrassing explanations and apologies to make. And what about the work she and Richard should have been doing at that minute? She realized Tom was talking and she hadn't been paying attention.

"...Dave's going to take you out in one of the four-wheel drives while I finish up here." Tom rested his hand gently on Darian's shoulder, and that touch came closer to pushing her over the edge of tears than anything else that had happened. "There's a phone in the truck. If Jason turns up here I'll call you right away."

At that moment Richard returned and cleared his throat conspicuously. "Dee, I've taken care of the dog thing." He glanced at his watch and gave her a helpless, unhappy look.

"Oh, God, Richard, I'm sorry. I know we have to get back."

"I want to stay and help, but—"

Tom glanced from Darian to Richard. "Did you two ride out together?"

Darian nodded miserably. "We've got pleadings due on Monday and staff in the office waiting for us. We should have been headed back to Austin by now."

Tom was already beginning to back away, but he glanced at Richard. "Why don't you head on back? I'll be happy to drive Darian and Jason to Austin. I'm sure Darian will worry less if she knows you're getting started."

"Would you? That'd be great," Richard said. He looked back at Darian and gave her an I-don't-know-what-else-to-do shrug.

"We really appreciate this," Darian said, feeling worse with every passing moment. Not only was she a neglectful mother and an imposition on her host, now one of her associates had to do her work for her. *You just can't do anything right, can you?*

"You need anything out of the truck?" Richard asked. "No? Okay, I'm off. I'll be there all night, so feel free to join me in progress."

"I'll be there," Darian said with a firmness and conviction she wished she felt. Once this stupid business was taken care of, she intended to redouble her efforts at the firm. She'd make it up to Richard and their client.

For the next two hours, Darian jounced around Clearpool Ranch in Dave Alexander's olive-green four-wheel drive. Every so often they'd stop the motor and stand outside, listening for the sound of the Landskimmer's little engine. A kind of numb misery settled over her, and Dave eventually quit trying to reassure her with cheerful platitudes. By five-thirty, the sky was turning pink and violet, and a spectacular sunset was gathering force over the low, rugged hills of the Cypress Creek Valley.

Dave phoned the ranch from the truck, and the woman who answered said neither Jason nor the puppy had turned up. The auction was over and the dance would be starting soon. Since daylight was failing, Dave suggested they go back to the ranch for flashlights. Darian also had to decide if she wanted to involve law enforcement since it was getting dark. And cold.

Twenty minutes later, they walked into the kitchen of the Old Place. Sheriff Joe Bob McAllister, Carl Thibodeux, Tony Royer and several other employees of Tom's were sitting at the long, scarred kitchen table. Someone had made an urn of coffee, and the dark, strong smell of it filled the room. When Darian walked in, one of the men at the table pushed his chair back, and the legs shrieked on the floor. She flinched.

"Ah, coffee," Dave said. "Sit down, Darian, and I'll get you a cup. Where's Tom?"

"He's on his way," Sheriff McAllister said. "Just had to say goodbye to some people."

The sight of the men sitting casually around the kitchen table made Darian almost choke with anger and frustration. She was beginning to lose the fight with a mother's panic for her missing child.

The sun had fallen quickly, and although its pale violet penumbra still glowed in the west like the lights of a distant city, hard little stars were beginning to glitter high overhead, and a fingernail moon had cut a bright slice in the navy night. Darian shivered. Her son was alone in the dark, and she wanted every able-bodied man within a hundred miles out there, on hands and knees if necessary, looking for him.

Someone opened a door, and the distant sound of music came in along with the rumble of laughter and happy conversation. Nearly a hundred people had stayed to dance to the country swing band, and the sides of the tent had been drawn up. Looking out the kitchen window, Darian could see the light, warm and yellow as butter. The couples whirled by, dancing with happy oblivion.

For some reason the sight made her more desperate than ever. She hated seeing all those happy, dancing people; she hadn't seen Jason for more than six hours. Tears were already scalding the back of her throat, and she knew soon she'd be unable to hold them in. *He's just a little boy and he's out there all alone. Something terrible has happened to him. This is all my fault.* At that moment the kitchen door swung open and Tom walked in. For some reason, the sight of him—tall, purposeful and in charge—made her feel more like crying than ever. "Tom" was all she managed. Her voice broke a little, and she cleared her throat.

"Good. Everybody's here," he said, looking around the room with businesslike satisfaction. "Diego has the horses saddled up. Tony, you take my four-wheel drive and go up to Poolwood Story. I don't think he'd go that far, but why don't you go look anyway? Thanks, buddy. If you want to hold on a second, Dominga is getting some thermoses together."

He took off his hat and laid it, crown down, on the counter. His thick hair was reddish brown and a little too long over his collar, and his hat had made an indentation just above his nape. He turned around and held a mug under the steaming spout of the coffee urn. "I'll go west because that's where most of the dry beds are, and I know that land the best. Mike and Dave are driving up to the Clearpool Source. We know he's not on the road. Nobody drove an ATV out the gate. Right, Rudy?"

A wiry little man wearing a red plaid shirt, a sleeveless down vest and a sweat-stained ShurGro Feed cap stood up straight and tried to look important. "No, sir. I been at that there gate all day. Ain't nobody droven one of them things past me."

Tom turned to Darian and gave her a reassuring smile. "Look," he said, and opened his jacket. Hanging inside his shoulder holster was a cellular phone. "High-tech posse, ma'am."

Darian laughed a little but it came out like a sob. "I want to go," she blurted.

Tom raised a skeptical eyebrow. "Can you ride?"

"Of course. Anyway, the horse does all the work, right?"

Tom didn't answer right away but gazed steadily into her eyes. The men passed looks among themselves and stood up noisily. Joe Bob gave Tom a dark look and began to divide the men into groups. "Excuse me, but how many horses did you say you've got ready?"

"Eight. Just leave me Clyde. You can take anything else in the barn." He turned back toward Darian. "Actually, I'm afraid there's quite a lot to riding, Darian. Especially in the hill country. And tonight, there's almost no moon. You've got to know what you're doing."

"But I can't stay here and just wait. I have to do something." The entreaty in her voice sounded pathetic, but she didn't care.

He tilted his head to the side, assessing, maybe weighing the possibilities. "Come on then. I think we can fix you up."

Ten minutes later, she was walking toward the barn wearing a pair of Daphne Steinbuck's jeans hitched up with one of Tom's belts. He'd given her one of his sweaters to wear, too, and she could smell him on it—pine, leather and some old-fashioned kind of soap or shaving cream.

By the time they reached the barn, all the others were gone except Rudy who stood alone in the yellow light spilling from the open doors. He held two horses—one neat little black mare with a white snip, like a dollop of whipped cream, on the end of her nose; the other was the biggest, ugliest horse Darian had ever seen.

"This is Clyde," Tom said, as he took the reins from the shorter man. "He's a Percheron."

An unenthusiastic "Mmm" was all she could manage. The animal was enormous and heavily muscled with loose, dappled gray hide and pale, grizzled mane that stood up from his forelock and neck like broom straw. He looked like a sleepy, disagreeable old man wearing oversize pajamas and a bad wig. He didn't look friendly at all.

"Look at the size of his feet," Tom said. "That's where you can really see he's cold-blooded—you know, a draft horse."

The animal's hooves were the size of dinner plates and a huge curtain of coarse, white hair fell from well above his ankles all the way to the ground. He looked as if he had all four feet in lampshades.

Tom gave Darian a pleasant brisk smile. "Ready?"

"Mmm," she repeated.

"Got your flashlight, Rudy? Good. You know the east pasture and the pecan grove? Why don't you go that way? If you don't find anything, call me and you can come help us."

The little man nodded, vaulted onto the mare's back without ever touching the stirrups. Then he turned her on her square haunches and galloped away into the dark. Clyde heaved his enormous gray head around to watch, sighed, cocked his hip and swung his head back around.

"Come around this side," Tom said. "I'll get on first. Like this, see? Put your left foot in here and then up." He swung into the saddle easily, and Darian had to crane her head far back to look up at him.

"It's too high," she said softly. "I don't think my leg will reach."

"Yes it will. Give me your hand and you just swing up behind me."

The animal stood with stonelike patience while Tom leaned over and took her hand. As soon as Darian's foot was in the stirrup, he hauled her up behind him. Clyde grunted and swished his tail hard enough to smack against her leg. Darian hadn't been on a horse since camp twenty years earlier. She didn't remember them being nearly as wide or tall as Clyde.

"Hold on around my waist," Tom said. "That's it. Just until you get used to the way he moves," he added, and patted her hand. "Hup," he said quietly, and the huge animal lumbered off. "Try to relax and you won't bounce. Hold on now."

Tom's jacket was unbuttoned, and Darian's hands pressed hard against his sides. She could feel the easy flex of muscle, warm and solid, as his body moved effortlessly with the motion of the horse. Her chin hit him right between his shoulder blades.

They passed to the south of the tent, and soft western swing music and the mellow sound of happy people followed them into the velvet darkness. For the first time since Jason had disappeared, Darian let her control slip. A hot tear slid down her cheek, and she tried not to sniff out loud. Tom's left arm settled over Darian's, and he let his hand cover hers and patted her fingers. "It'll be okay," he said. "Please don't worry."

In moments they left the ranch behind, but the light followed them and that comforted Darian. If she could see the light, Jason could, too. Clyde's enormous shoes clicked on little rocks in the footing, and when Tom turned him to canter straight across country, his hooves thudded against the ground like distant pile drivers.

"If he went this way," Tom said, "we should find him pretty soon. It's mostly flat, except for a few creek beds. Look, an owl."

Above them a silent, gray shadow floated effortlessly. The head was huge and round as a softball. The night bird followed them for a few curious moments then tilted away in the darkness. "Are there a lot of... animals out here?" Darian asked.

Again Tom pressed her hand with his. "Well, we've got deer out the wazzoo, possums, raccoons, armadillo and fox. And there's still the occasional mangy coyote, but that's about it. Lots of rabbits, of course, but nothing dangerous. The bears and wolves are long gone."

"How about snakes?" Darian asked, and curled her toes inside her boots.

Tom didn't answer aloud, but Darian felt his thighs tighten. Clyde gave an angry grunt and heaved himself forward, his huge, rounded hips rocking Darian against Tom's back with muscular force. She had to tighten her arms around Tom's waist.

"Do you mind if I ask you a personal question?" he asked suddenly.

"Not at all. What is it?"

He hesitated for a moment. "Where's Jason's dad?"

"Joel? Seattle, I think," Darian answered. "I'm not really sure. We haven't heard from him in years. He signed away his parental rights when Jason was four because he didn't want to pay child support." She was glad she couldn't see Tom's face; she hated the looks people gave her when she talked about Joel. "He was—is a folk singer. I married him my first year at U.T. when I was young and stupid. At the time I just knew it was true love."

"He didn't want a...family?"

"The way he put it was, 'You know I love you guys, but this family gig is really starting to strangle my creative energy.' He went on the road one September and never came back."

Tom muttered a curse. "Sorry," he said. "That was crude."

"Yes, but my sentiments exactly. I don't mind for me, but it's so hard for Jason. I blame Joel for this. Jason's a good kid, and really smart, but he needs a father. He needs *his* father," she corrected. "I think he's feeling, you know, abandoned."

"I know people desert their kids," Tom said, his voice harsh with disgust. "I just don't get it. How can you have a son, a family, and just walk away?"

"You'd be surprised how easy it is for some people," Darian replied.

They galloped on in the darkness, and the wind dragged at Darian's hair and burned her eyes. She was glad to have Tom's body to shield hers from the cold air. She didn't feel steady on the horse and kept her arms wrapped tightly around his torso. He was humming, but she felt rather than heard it—the faint vibration under her fingers. It seemed odd to touch someone so intimately. How many years had it been since she'd had her arms around a man for any reason? Good God, she thought, it had been eight years. Where had time gone?

The rugged land began to rise around them, and the little stands of juniper became denser and punctuated by pale boulders or the ragged tops of oaks and black walnut trees. They rode for about half an hour, and then Tom pulled the horse to a stop and fumbled with something at the front of the saddle. In a moment he lifted his arm and a bright column of light sliced through the darkness in front of them. Darian hadn't seen that he had a flashlight tethered to the saddle.

"He might have come this way, but I'm no expert on tracks so I can't tell how old these tire marks are or what kind of vehicle made 'em. Damn," he muttered. He sighed, swung the beam of light at the stand of trees and nudged the horse into a walk. They rode in silence for a few moments, and Darian could once again feel tears of frustration gathering in her throat. Vivid nightmare scenes played in her mind in agonizing detail. Missing-person reports. Milk-carton photographs. The deafening silence of a child's empty room.

Tom stood up in the stirrups and aimed the flashlight first on one side, then the other. He settled back in the saddle with a disappointed sigh. "Darian, do you feel safe enough to let go with one hand and hold the flashlight? I'm afraid we might miss something."

"Sure, but don't start going fast without warning me." She knew the wobble in her voice revealed how emotional she was becoming, but if Tom noticed he didn't say anything.

For the next four hours they carefully combed every dry creek bed and any likely-looking stand of trees. Tom never once complained or said anything disparaging about Jason. Hour after hour Clyde trudged onward, his heavy feet thudding against the ground with plodding rhythm. Three times they stopped to rest, and each time Darian found it more difficult to climb back up on the horse. Finally, close to midnight, they reached the farthest, most rugged point of Clearpool Ranch, almost twelve miles from the house.

"Do you think we should call out some more?" Darian asked.

"Couldn't hurt. You want me to this time?"

"Would you?" Tom's voice would be louder and not as raw and high-pitched as hers had become. She felt his chest expand as he took a deep breath, but before any sound emerged, he suddenly yanked the reins. Darian was thrown forward roughly against his back, and had to snatch at him to steady herself. "What is it? Tom? What?"

"I ... I'm not sure."

He aimed the flashlight at a small clump of cedars, and at first Darian couldn't tell what had caught his attention. But then she saw the skinned bark and snapped branches. Something had gone careening through the trees and torn away their bark. Sap, like sticky amber blood, dripped slowly from fresh, pale wounds. Clyde grunted and broke into a ponderous trot.

The gorge was invisible until you reached the edge, and then it opened suddenly like a ragged mouth. A new gash, dark and oozing moisture, had been plowed over the lip of the ravine. Below that, creek overflow and rushing water from flash floods had washed away the topsoil and left only naked rocks and tough vegetation clinging wretchedly to the stony walls.

At the bottom, lying on its side, was the Hummie. One headlight was shattered and the left fender was torn off. It stared up at Darian like a ruined face with one blind eye and one empty socket.

The blood began to roar in her ears and she knew Tom was speaking, but she couldn't hear the words. Someone was screaming her son's name, and for a moment Darian was vaguely aware that she was no longer on the horse, but beneath him and looking up at the coarse, matted hair of his belly. She was distantly cognizant of one enormous, iron-shod hoof held directly over her rib cage but poised, almost delicately, above her in midair. Then the ground tumbled beneath her by itself and she saw the trees and rocks rushing past while a lunatic beam of light wagged madly around her, then went out.

"Jason," she sobbed. "Where are you? Baby, please answer me. Can you hear me? It's Mommy." At the bottom of the ravine, she scrabbled frantically at the cold, slick metal and clammy upholstery, feeling for his little body and sobbing out his name.

Then Tom was behind her in the dark. One arm circled her waist pulling her away, the other wrapped around her shoulders. He was turning her around. "...not here. Darian, listen to me. Jason's not here."

Her heart hammered so violently it made her chest ache. "What? Let me go. What did you say?"

"Look. See? Jason is gone. The dog is gone. They must have walked away." The meager light from the moon and stars dusted everything around her in ash-colored light, but Tom was right. She could see. Just as he said, they were alone.

The backwash of light framed his face, and Darian saw he'd lost his hat, and his hair hung across his forehead. She stared at his silhouette for the space of three heartbeats, and for those moments all she heard was the whistle of her own breathing. Then she heard a sound—so foreign at that terrible moment she almost broke into hysterical laughter.

A telephone was ringing.

Chapter Three

They both froze like deer caught in headlights. Tom recovered first and jammed his hand into his jacket. "Hello. Yeah, at least thirty minutes. We're at the northwest corner in the runoff gorge. He did? Thank God. When? Where was—"

"Did they find him?" Darian asked. "Is he—"

"Mrs. Conroy wants to talk to her son, where is— Oh. Okay, I'll tell her. Can you send Rudy up the logging road with the trailer? Thanks, Joe Bob." He snapped the phone shut. "Jason's fine. Rudy found him hiding in the barn. He couldn't come to the phone right then because he was outside with the sheriff. Something about the dog."

Darian felt her blood rise to the surface of her skin in a hot tingling rush of emotion. *Jason's fine. They found him hiding in the barn.* She wanted to shout thanks to heaven. She'd been so afraid he was dead. For one horrible instant she could even have sworn she'd seen his body under the ATV. Then Tom's words registered more fully. "Hiding? Did you say hiding?"

"In the barn," Tom repeated quietly.

Darian's eyes were becoming adjusted to the dark but still she couldn't quite make out Tom's expression. Part of her was glad. That meant he couldn't see hers, either.

"The mare threw Rudy off, and he had to walk back to get her. He found Jason in one of the stalls with the puppy. Apparently he'd been there for a few hours."

"When did they find him?"

"He said about eleven."

"What? That's more than an hour ago? Why didn't anyone—"

"Nobody at the house had the number of this phone. They had to wait until Dave came back."

As Tom's words began to sink in, Darian's surge of joy subsided. She thought of the hours she'd spent terrified for Jason's life. *Hiding in the barn.* The men who'd spent hours searching for him. The eight-hundred-dollar puppy and wrecked ATV. *Hiding in the barn.*

She wanted very much to think calmly and methodically. She wanted to be reasonable and mature and respond effectively to this challenging situation.

She wanted to wring Jason's neck. "May I use the phone, please? I want to talk to my son."

The phone chirped to life when Tom flipped it open. He held it out toward her, and the glowing buttons added a green tinge to the gray moonlight. "Just press the talk button," he said. "The number is five-five-five-twenty-twenty. I'm sure somebody'll be glad to go outside and get him."

Darian's hands shook, and she couldn't seem to dial the number correctly. After two failed attempts, punctuated with words she rarely said aloud, she took a deep breath and pressed the "off" button. She paused for a moment, then closed the phone.

Her emotions weren't completely in focus yet, and she realized she needed some time to think. Jason was fine. She smiled grimly. *He's outside with Joe Bob*. He's probably having a really pleasant tête-à-tête with the sheriff. "Actually, I think I'll hold off for a few minutes." She handed the phone back to Tom.

She was almost certain she saw a smile flicker across Tom's face. She was positive she heard him mutter, "Good."

"Wait here for a minute while I see if I can find the flashlight." He turned and scrambled up the side of the ravine. In a few moments the light flicked on. He clambered back down and stood over the ATV. "Can you hold this while I try to turn this thing over?"

"Oh, of course. Oh, dear. What a mess. How bad is it?"

Tom shrugged. "I don't know. Doesn't look like the axle is broken." He pushed the Hummie over onto its tires and it bounced upright like a tough little soldier— injured but still willing. When he turned the key the engine coughed once, then sputtered to life. When Tom rotated the handle, the engine revved with undiminished power.

In spite of everything, Darian's spirits rose. "Well, can you believe that?"

"Who'd have thought it? Maybe just some paint and a new headlight is all it'll need." He reached down again and the Hummie growled, almost reluctantly, into silence. "There's an easy way out of here farther down, but I think I'll let one of the guys try it in the morning." He stood up straight, took the flashlight from Darian and aimed it at the top of the ravine. "Rudy'll be here in about twenty minutes. You ready to climb back up?"

Darian glanced at the steep slope she'd scrambled down. It looked almost vertical. "Good grief. How did I, uh, did you see me—"

Tom chuckled wryly. "Don't ask me. One minute you were behind me on Clyde, and the next thing you were flying over the edge like Spiderman. Or Spiderwoman, I guess."

"I don't even remember climbing down."

"You didn't really climb. You mostly jumped."

"It's a wonder I didn't break something important."

He took a couple of steps up the rocks, then turned and reached his hand out to her. "You're gonna feel it tomorrow."

Darian took a deep breath. "I think I'm beginning to feel it now." She took the hand he offered her and let him haul her up the steep slope. In ten minutes they were both panting and standing beside Clyde, who stood with patient boredom where Tom had left him.

"You didn't tie him up," Darian said when she noticed the reins trailing on the ground. "Why didn't he run back home?"

Tom looped the reins over the horse's neck and noisily patted him. "Most horses would, but not this guy. You're a good boy, aren't you, Clyde? You wouldn't run home and leave your poor old master out here to walk home, would you?" The horse responded with a weary sigh and swung his head away morosely. Tom glanced at Darian. "He's crazy about me."

Darian laughed a little. "Oh yeah, I can tell."

"Good old Clyde," Tom said and swatted his horse affectionately.

"You know," Darian said thoughtfully as her breath slowed, "when I jumped off I fell under him and I think I remember this gigantic hoof waving around right over me—"

"But he stopped?"

"That's right. At least I think I remember that."

"I thought I felt him hesitate. He's a good 'un, all right."

"Tom."

"Mmm-hmm."

"I want you to know I really appreciate everything you and your friends did for me today. I don't know what I would have done—"

"Stop right there," he said. "I'm glad—we're all glad—to help. I know there's nothing I can say to make you feel better right now, but let me tell you, everyone, especially me, was happy to do it. Like I said earlier, these charity soirees bore me out of my skull, and I was just glad to have an excuse to disappear."

Darian sighed. "Thanks for saying so." Now that she knew Jason was safe and sound, her other worries threatened to overwhelm her. How much would it cost to repair the ATV? What was she going to do with the dog? What were the partners going to say? She sighed again. And what about Richard and the work she should have been doing at that very moment?

As they stood quietly in the clearing, waiting for Rudy, Darian became acutely aware of aches and pains she'd been too upset to notice earlier. The muscles along the insides of her legs were on fire, and her arms ached from clinging to Tom for so many hours. Both palms were grazed from her trip into the ravine, and she felt little bits of dirt and grass burning in fine cuts. There was also a kink in her spine, and she thought she'd pulled something in one shoulder. She pressed her hands against the small of her back and rocked from side to side.

"Sore?" Tom asked.

"All over."

"There's a hot tub at the house, but it might do more harm than good."

Darian sighed. "I'm so exhausted, I'd probably drown myself."

"I was thinking," Tom said slowly. "I know we planned to drive back to Austin tonight, but you and Jason are more than welcome to stay here. There're at least six empty bedrooms."

"Thanks. That's something to think about." Darian reached up and patted Clyde absently. Maybe Tom was right. It would be around one o'clock by the time they got back to the ranch. Then there was the matter of dealing with Jason and the sheriff and thanking everyone who had spent so many hours searching. And Tom. He would be exhausted, too. It wouldn't be very nice to expect him or one of his men to drive her all the way to Austin, then turn around and drive back to Wimberley.

"Actually, I'd like to accept your invitation. To stay over, I mean."

"Good," he said. "That's good."

Darian thought he sounded almost elated, and for a moment she wondered if he was that glad not to have to make the drive, or if there could be more to it than that. Before she could really analyze his reaction, she heard the sound of an engine.

"Here comes Rudy," Tom said. "We'll have Clyde loaded up in just a minute and we can head on back."

They arrived back at the house in less than half an hour.

Sheriff McAllister was sitting in his car and talking on his radio, and when they pulled up he stood and closed the door, then touched his hat. "Mrs. Conroy. Your boy's in the house with Dominga. She washed him up and made him a sandwich." Then he glanced at Tom. "Do you want me to write up anything about this? Make any kind of charge, I mean?"

Darian saw a flash of irritation cross Tom's face. "That won't be necessary, Joe Bob. Mrs. Conroy will take care of it, I think."

There was no mistaking the look of disapproval on the sheriff's face. "Up to you," he muttered. "I'm heading back then. I'll talk to you tomorrow." He nodded at Darian, but didn't really look her squarely in the face. "Mrs. Conroy."

"Thanks for your help, Sheriff," she said tiredly. "Thank you for everything. Is there anything I need to—"

"Not a thing, ma'am. Good night to you. Tom."

When they walked into the kitchen, the first person Darian saw was Dominga Villareal, Tom's housekeeper. Tom had introduced Darian to her earlier. The stout, middle-aged woman stood at the sink drying dishes while six or seven men sat drinking mugs of coffee around the huge scrubbed table. Their conversation died when Darian arrived in the doorway, and when Dominga looked up and saw Darian, she slid her dark eyes toward Jason and covered her mouth with a moist, nut-brown hand.

He sat, small and pale, at the end of the table—his hair damp and slicked back with an unfamiliar parting. A sandwich, ridiculously thick with sliced roast beef, lay half-eaten on the plate in front of him, and a tumbler of milk stood perfectly centered on a coaster. He'd been swinging his legs but stopped instantly when he saw his mother.

Despite her exhaustion, the instant Darian saw him her anger returned and with it the choking sensation of unshed tears. Calling on every bit of courtroom control she'd ever accumulated, she turned to Tom. His expression was inscrutable. "Is there a place where Jason and I can speak privately?" Although she turned away to face Tom, the grinding sound of chair legs told her Jason had risen to follow.

Tom nodded and led them to the end of a long hallway, then opened the door and stood aside. The bedroom was decorated with scarlet Mexican rugs and heavy pine furniture. A Brahma bull gazed solemnly down from a portrait over the bed, and nubby, cream-colored drapes were opened slightly to reveal tall, many-paned windows. An open door led through to a little private bathroom. Tom stood at the door for just a moment, then shook his head slightly as if he'd decided against what he'd intended to say. "I'll leave you two alone."

"Thank you," Darian said, and turned to face her son.

Tom closed the door quietly when he left. As he walked down the hall, he tried to imagine what Darian would say. And do. He knew what his own mother would have done. He'd be leaning across the bed by now, getting intimately acquainted with a willow switch while, through a flood of Irish tears, she called all the saints in heaven to witness his wickedness. His heartless cruelty. Her undeserved suffering. He smiled ruefully. People did things differently nowadays. Especially people like Darian Conroy.

What an interesting woman, he thought. From the minute he'd seen her striding into the tent, beautiful and businesslike, with her blond hair swinging like a thick tassel, he'd thought she seemed special. Despite those silly green cowboy boots.

He wasn't surprised to find out she was with Sternwell and Haig, even though he'd never seen her in all his trips to the firm. But that wasn't really surprising since she worked in the trial department, not oil and gas. He smiled a little. She was a typical trial lawyer—determined, unafraid and hell-bent on keeping her emotions concealed. And what brains she had.

She sure didn't seem to be very impressed with you, though.

He smiled ruefully. It wasn't very often he couldn't charm a lady. Especially when he tried as hard to be charming as he had with her.

But that was because she was worried sick about her son, he told himself.

Hah! Shovel that load off on somebody else. Before all that—when you were together in the house, she wasn't that interested. She's got her own life—a son and a career—and believe it or not she just isn't particularly awe-struck by you, old buddy.

Tom frowned. Maybe that was true. From everything she said, her life was full and hectic with her job and the *pro bono* work she did for indigent women. And her son.

And what about that boy? There was something strange going on there. Tom had confidence in his judgment of character. He'd sized up plenty of people—men, women and children—and Jason Conroy was not some spoiled brat or a little punk who'd gone joyriding just to be rebellious. He seemed to be a serious kid. Smart and not scared at all. Even when they'd walked into the kitchen, he looked straight into his mother's eyes—just glad to see her. No head ducking, no mumbled apologies or hysterics or sudden begging. He just stood up and followed her.

Tom stopped for a moment and glanced back down the hallway toward the room where he'd left them. He wondered for a moment if he should put Darian closer to her son, but changed his mind and opened the door at his left. He started a fire in the fireplace and turned back the bed, then glanced around. There wouldn't be anything for her to wear to sleep in. When he pulled open the chest of drawers, the first thing he saw was one of his old T-shirts, folded perfectly and smelling of whatever it was Dominga put in the wash.

He picked up the shirt and smiled to himself. He liked the idea of Darian sleeping in his T-shirt. He wondered what her legs were shaped like. They were certainly long. Even without her boots she was probably five-nine or ten.

What the hell are you thinking of, you dog? She's been worried sick about her son for hours, and here you are thinking about her legs? He dropped the shirt on the bed, closed the door and walked out.

When he walked into the kitchen, the other men smiled and nudged each other companionably. "I'll bet somebody's gonna need a cushion to sit on for a couple days," Arnold Rudman said.

"Oooh, the lickin' my mama would give me," Rudy said, and patted his skinny backside with both hands. The other men laughed noisily, and swapped stories about their own boyhood escapades and subsequent whippings.

"What d'you think, Tomas?" Dominga asked, her eyes saucerlike. "Will she beat the *niño?*"

"Dunno," said Tom, and shrugged. He smiled at her. "But I don't think so."

The room had taken on the tired satisfaction that marked the end of a successful hunt. Tom sat at the table with his legs outstretched and enjoyed a scalding cup of strong coffee. Eventually someone suggested they have a drink, and he opened a bottle of good Kentucky bourbon. They all stood and drank a shot to their success. Other hunts had not ended so well—some in the emergency room, or the police station. Or worse.

For the next half hour, he enjoyed the company of his friends and neighbors until, one by one, they stood, shook hands and headed for their homes. Tom walked outside and watched as engine after engine fired up, lights blinked on and went bouncing over the rumpled land until they hit the graded driveway. Since Dominga had gone to bed, he stacked the mugs in the sink along with the shot glasses and waited for Darian to come back.

When she did, he could see that she had washed her face and tied her hair back again. She looked pale, and had dark smudges beneath her eyes, but still he was again struck with her scrubbed good looks. Her undeniable good breeding and sensible gracefulness.

She glanced around as she entered the room. "Did everybody go? I didn't get a chance to—"

"Don't worry about it," he interrupted. "There's plenty of time for thank-yous. Coffee?"

"I'd rather have a shot of that bourbon."

He smiled. "Good idea. I'll join you."

The second mouthful of rich brown liquor made a warm path down Tom's throat, and he licked his lips and tilted his head to the side. "That's good stuff."

"Mmm," Darian said, and set her glass down carefully. "Tom, I know I've said it before, but I can't tell you how much I appreciate everything you've done today."

"Please try," he said, and grinned at her.

She did laugh a little at the joke, but her smile didn't reach her eyes. "No, really. You were wonderful. Your friends, the sheriff, everyone. And the party, I hope we didn't—"

"Oh, enough. I told you earlier, I hate these things. I just provide the place and a few go-withs. Other people do all the work. This gave me something interesting to do while all those boring rich people rubbed shoulders and acted generous."

This time the smile did reach her eyes.

"How's Jason?"

Her gaze fell. "All right, I suppose. Worried about the dog."

"What's wrong with her?"

"When…" Her voice trailed away for a moment, and Tom could see she was beginning to struggle with tears again. "When he saw that he wasn't going to be able to stop the ATV before it went over the edge, he threw her clear before he jumped off. Now it seems there's something wrong with one of her paws."

"I don't know what you plan to do with her, but I'll be glad to take her to the vet tomorrow."

She smiled wearily. "Thanks."

He wanted to pull her into his arms. If he'd ever seen a woman in need of being held, it was Darian. Still, something told him he had to be careful. He sure didn't want her to get the wrong idea. He lifted the coffeepot and poured himself a mug. "You want to change your mind?"

"Sure. Thanks." She took the mug he offered her, cupped her hands around it and held it close to her chest. "Jason…he said he wants to talk to you in the morning. He wanted to tonight, but after he had a bath, he just couldn't stay awake."

"I'd be glad to talk to him."

"You know what he said? He says he didn't mean to steal her, he meant to rescue her."

"From what?"

"That Mr. Winfield. From being a hunting dog and then being a puppy mill."

Tom's eyes felt grainy, and he rubbed them with a finger and thumb. "Well, to tell you the truth, that doesn't surprise me. Luther Winfield's a disagreeable old windbag, and the only reason he comes to charity events is so he can wrangle some kind of tax deduction." Darian was staring into her coffee, so he couldn't see if what he said was making any difference to her.

"About the Hummie—"

"You know," he interrupted. "I've been thinking about that and I want to propose something to you."

When she looked up into his face and licked her lips slightly, Tom felt suddenly unsure—as if he'd just stepped out on a diving platform to find he was much higher than he'd realized. Darian gazed at him steadily with huge hazel eyes fringed with thick long eyelashes— even more compelling and dramatic for their lack of makeup. Like her mouth with its wide full lips that didn't quite close even when she wasn't speaking.

"Yes?"

What a pretty woman. "I'd like to let Jason work off whatever it costs to have the Hummie fixed."

Her eyes widened. "Here? Doing what?"

"There's plenty of work to be done around here. Stalls to be cleaned. Hay baling, polishing harness, livestock to feed and tend. And that's not counting the yard work. It takes two riding mowers just to keep the grounds around the house in shape—"

"Thank . . . thanks for offering, but I don't know—"

"And if it's a matter of transportation, somebody from the ranch goes into Austin almost every day. I can arrange to have him picked up after school on Friday and brought back home to you on Sunday evening. And he'll be well supervised. Dominga's always in the house, and her husband and sons live on the ranch, too. After his work is done, he'd have boys close to his own age to spend time with."

She looked up at him. "That's an interesting idea, but don't you think it sounds more like a reward than a punishment? I mean, playing with livestock and driving tractors in the hill country?"

"Well, that's true, he may enjoy it, but the work is hard, and he'll really earn the money he gets paid. This way he can honestly pay for what he's done. And if he learns to love the land and gets some experience doing a hard day's work—so much the better, don't you think? I mean, I'm no psychiatrist, but I do know that a fellow needs to see that there's something he can do to make up for his . . . mistakes." He had to make her understand how important this could be. He didn't want to dredge up old stories, but he would if he was forced to.

Her gaze slid away, and he could see that she was thinking about it. She chewed the corner of her mouth a little, and her pretty eyebrows slanted together.

Say yes. Just say yes. I can see you want to. "And, of course, you'd be welcome to spend as much time out here as you'd like."

She rolled her eyes. "You don't know how much I'd love to. It's so beautiful out here, but with my schedule . . ."

"Are you afraid his schoolwork will suffer?"

"Oh, no. It's not that. Jason's gifted. The only problem he's ever had with the work has been keeping him challenged in school. That's the whole reason I send him to Fullingham."

"Do you think he'd be interested in the idea?"

She raised her thumb up to her mouth as if she were going to chew the nail, then she seemed to remember herself and folded her arms. "I'm not sure. He's never done anything like this. Before I would have said no way, because he's been going on weekend trips with his school. But, of course, that's out for now." She glanced up and he could see she regretted what she had to say. "He's been suspended from extracurricular activities."

"Oh. Too bad."

Darian fell silent, and Tom could see there was more on her mind than just considering his offer. Her eyes took on a sheen, and she kept swallowing. Everything—the set of her shoulders, the way she pressed her lips together—all showed that she was fighting to maintain composure. So, it's finally hitting home, he thought.

"You see," she said thickly, "I'm really trying hard to do the right thing for him, and at this moment your suggestion sounds like a good idea, but I don't know how clearly I'm thinking. Jason's the most important thing in the world to me, but lately I seem to be doing everything wrong. But I know you can imagine how a parent—a single parent especially—feels about her only child."

Tom felt a familiar, dull ache, like the pain from a bone broken years ago. He was so accustomed to it he hardly noticed it anymore. "Yes. I can...imagine."

She put down her cup, squeezed her eyes closed and rubbed them with her fingers. When she spoke, her voice rasped with emotion. "When I put him to bed just now, he fell asleep right away. He was so tired." She cleared her throat. "Funny, isn't it, how the littlest things can get to you? He sleeps on his stomach and he had his hand up on the pillow close to his face. Like this." She cleared her throat again.

A strand of her hair had come loose, and Tom wanted to reach up and push it back behind her ear. No, he *needed* to reach up and touch her.

He realized he was thrumming with need. Not a sexual urgency, but something different. He needed to comfort her. To be tall and strong as a seawall and hold back the tide of exhaustion and despair he saw her trying to endure alone. Let me do this for you, he wanted to say. Let me be who I am. What I am. Just let me help you. He didn't speak, but put his own cup down, and moved a step closer to her. He could have reached out and touched her then but something said *not yet*.

She was speaking again. "His little shoulder is so…so perfect. And his hand and his forehead. I wanted to pick him up, like I did when he was a baby. If something would have happened to him I…I—"

Now. He didn't say anything, he merely pulled her to him and let her cry. Her arms clamped around him, and her silent sobs thudded through her. He shook his head. She even cried with self-control, obviously so as not to impose her emotion on him. "Let it go," he murmured. "No point in trying to hold back."

She fit perfectly against him. Tall and curved and long-limbed. He stroked her hair and breathed slowly—oddly aware of the rise and fall of his own chest against her body. Her tears didn't last long, and he could tell when she became disgusted with herself by the way she wiped her face roughly with the back and heel of her hand.

"I'm being stupid," she said, and stepped away. She didn't look up. "I'm sorry."

"No. Not stupid. Nothing like that. Who wouldn't cry? After all, 'Here is my son who was lost and is found. Who was dead and is alive.'" He leaned against the tile counter, giving her space. "I'd be out of my head with relief."

She wouldn't look up at him, but shrugged slightly and made some quiet little sound in the ragged wake of her tears.

"You must be exhausted," he said. "Why don't I show you where you're sleeping."

She looked at him then—a fleeting look of gratitude in her stormy, reddened eyes. She nodded. "That'd be nice."

When he led her down the hall, it seemed to him that the house was listening to them—observant and accepting. She was delighted by the fire in her room, and she thanked him again. At the door, she even stood on her tiptoes and kissed his cheek, and her long, cool fingers trailed for a brief instant against the skin of her neck.

Later he turned off the lights in the kitchen and walked outside before turning in for what was left of the night. His breath frosted in the air, and the twittering and calls of night creatures rustled around him, unseen but familiar.

He touched the place on his cheek where she had kissed him, and gazed toward the corner of the house where he knew she slept. He stood thinking and remembering until the light in her window went dark, and then, smiling to himself, he took himself to sleep in one of the guest rooms.

Chapter Four

Darian woke to the smells of coffee and frying bacon. She squinted as she turned over in the bed and blazing sunlight fell across her face. Two walls were almost completely made up of long windows facing south and east, and morning light streamed in through the curtains. She groaned when she sat up. Everything ached.

Turning painfully, she glanced at the clock. A little before seven. She'd be back in Austin and at the office by nine-thirty.

"Are you awake, Mom?" Jason's voice called tentatively from the hallway.

"Sure. Come on in."

The handle turned and the door opened slightly, but it was a long moment before it swung wide. Jason, his scrubbed face happy and proud, walked in carrying a tray heaped with coffee, toast, grapefruit, and the paper.

She gave him a wary smile. "Thank you, sweetheart. That looks wonderful."

He set the tray down on the bed. "I told Dominga you like your coffee black and strong."

She opened her arms. "C'm'ere, you."

He fell against her and she breathed him in. The shampoo. Sunburned skin. Something nice in his clothes.

"Whose shirt?"

"It belongs to Eddie. He's Dominga's son. There's three boys. Dominga made us oatmeal."

"That's nice. Everyone else up?"

"Yeah, for a long time." Jason squirmed away and Darian sighed a little. She was surprised he'd let her hold him for even that long.

"Well, I guess I better shower and get dressed. Is Mr. Steinbuck around?"

"In the kitchen with the other guys."

"Would you run and tell him that I'll be ready in twenty minutes?" With one hand, she steadied the tray while she swung her legs over the edge of the bed. She winced.

"Are you okay, Mom?"

She leveled a hard look at him. "Just sore."

The joy evaporated from his face and his gaze dropped. "Uh, I'll go tell Mr. Steinbuck."

"Thanks, honey." As soon as he turned away, the guilt swept over her in a familiar cold wave. "Jason." But he'd already gone.

Darian hissed and grunted as she tiptoed across the cold hardwood floor and into the bathroom. She grumbled to herself the whole way. "Oooh. Ow. Stupid horse. Stupid kid. I don't know why I feel guilty. He's the one— ow, damn, that's hot."

The shower loosened her aching muscles a little, but after she dressed she still felt achy and uncomfortable. The skirt and blouse she'd worn the day before seemed limp and stale, and she had no makeup in her purse. By the time she'd done what she could with lipstick and her hairbrush and made it to the kitchen, the men were long gone and Dominga was clearing away the remains of a massive breakfast. From the pile of dishes, Darian saw that there had been at least ten people eating at the table that morning.

Dominga's round motherly face broke into an enormous smile when Darian walked through the door. "Good morning, Mrs. Conroy. Better today?"

"Much better, thanks. I...I'm looking for my son and Mr. Stein—"

"Outside," she said, waving toward the door with a dish towel. "They're all at the barn."

Darian found Jason and Tom sitting on the blades of some massive piece of farming equipment. The green-and-yellow tractor loomed over them, huge and silent, like some waiting piece of siege machinery. Jason was obviously enrapt by whatever Tom was saying, and at one point the man reached over and gave her son a rough hug and a gentle punch on the arm. The boy ducked his head, leaned into the masculine affection and thumped Tom gleefully with a skinny elbow—grinning hugely the whole time.

Male bonding. Before now, the expression had always seemed comical and somehow vaguely derogatory to her. But there was something touching and poignant about seeing the two of them—a grown man and a boy—together that way. Outdoors. Talking manly talk.

If only Jason had a father...but, that was a ridiculous way to think. Jason did have a father. He just didn't have a father who loved him.

Suddenly sad, Darian had to swallow the thickness in her throat. Jason had so little male presence in his life—

only teachers and coaches. All the men who took time to be with him were people Darian paid to be there.

She felt another familiar wave of guilt. If only she'd remarried. But there just wasn't time. Even if she wanted to—

"Well, look who's here. Good morning, Darian." Tom stood, smiling. He wore jeans again, a buttoned down shirt and a soft denim jacket. He looked good in the morning light, muscular and confident but relaxed. His hat shielded his eyes, but when he smiled, the squint lines showed anyway.

Darian smiled back. "And good morning to you."

"Did you sleep okay?"

"I slept fine. All the damage was done before I got in bed."

He chuckled slightly. "If you think you're sore today, just wait till tomorrow."

"Oh, well," she said, laughing a little. "That'll really give me something to look forward to—waddling into court like Gabby Hayes."

His smile lessened slightly. "You could never look like Gabby Hayes." He paused. "You're much too tall."

All three of them laughed then.

"All right for you." She clasped her hands together in front of her. "I hate to rush you, but I really need to head back to the city. Have you had a chance to see about the ATV yet? And the puppy? Is she okay?"

Tom tipped his head to the side. "Oh, of course. They're both in the barn, but, uh . . . could I talk to you for a minute, Darian? Alone?"

Before she had a chance to answer, Jason stood. "I'll go see Winnie." He looked at his mother. "If that's okay."

Darian suddenly had the feeling she was the last person to be informed of a plan already in motion, and Jason's angelic expression did nothing to alleviate her suspicion. "Who's Winnie?"

"The dog," Tom said.

"Be back in five minutes," Darian said. "Are you wearing your watch? Good."

"Five minutes," he yelped over his shoulder and tore off toward the barn.

Tom was grinning when he faced back toward her. "Have you had a chance to think about what we talked about?"

Darian looked down at the scuffed toes of her boots. Ruined, she thought absently, completely ruined. "Well, not really. I was so tired last night . . ."

"Actually, I thought that might have happened, and I was going to suggest this. Why don't I drive you back to Austin now? Rodrigo had a friend from town out all weekend, and he's going to be driving him back this evening. He could bring Jason home later—say about six-thirty. That way, Jason could spend the day with us and we could show him what he'd be doing if you agree to let him stay. You'd have the whole day to work without any distractions, and some time to think about letting him work off his debt."

Darian wanted to bite her nails, which annoyed her. She thought she'd long ago broken her old habit and found more suitable ways of coping with sadness or stress. She folded her arms. "Who is Rodrigo?"

"Dominga's oldest. He's a good boy. Eighteen. I've known him all his life, and he's been driving my cars for the past two years."

She needed more time to think, to sort out her jumbled thoughts. Too many things had happened in the past twenty-four hours, and confusing images and feelings swirled through her mind. Jason's latest trouble at school. The auction. Luther Winfield. The dog. The Hummie. "I don't know. I don't know," she muttered. "What about the ATV?"

"It's going to have to go to the shop, but it doesn't look too bad. A couple of hundred dollars at the most."

"Well, at least that's good news. And didn't...wasn't there something wrong with the puppy, too? Last night seems so fuzzy and it was—"

"She's got a badly bruised pad. Nothing serious. Rudy can take care of it."

So much to think about. So many things to take care of. The interrogatories she and Richard had to submit tomorrow. And what the hell was she going to do with a dog? "I don't know, Tom—"

"He wants to stay. I told him you might consider it, and he said he'd really like the chance to pay for the damage he caused." The corner of his mouth lifted in a grin. "That's quite a son you've got. He wanted to negotiate his hourly rate with me."

At first Darian felt a flash of irritation. Tom should have let her broach the subject first; Jason was her son. But then she remembered the way they had looked together. Two guys working it out man to man. Doing guy stuff. Tractors and horses and hunting dogs. Maybe this was just what Jason needed. She was certainly short on answers lately. Today would be a good test, too. Low risk. Only a few hours. If Jason hated it, well, they'd work out something else.

"You're sure you don't mind?"

His huge smile answered her. "I love having kids out here." He glanced around. "Well, anytime you're ready we can head to town."

Darian felt a little dizzy. She had the sudden thought that this was probably the way she made Dr. Bounds feel every time he called her in for one of his conferences. Oh, well, she thought. Maybe I am the one being bamboozled this time, but what the heck. It's only one day. What can it hurt?

This time Darian enjoyed the drive through the hill country. The road dipped down through high rocky walls and jumped across the wide, shallow creeks. She rolled down her window to enjoy the biting air and the sound of water chuckling over the flat white rocks.

Fall painted the hill country in contrasting colors—fading oaks and red-handed sycamores against the unchanging green of cedar and pine. The barren trees were black lace against the bright October sky, and high, thin clouds slowly faded in the crisp air.

For the first time she noticed the roadside stands selling pecans, fall vegetables and pumpkins heaped up on hay bales. Darian found herself humming along with the music on the stereo. "That music sounds familiar."

"It's Alex Lockhart," Tom said. "He was playing at the dance." He glanced at her. "Sorry, if that's an unpleasant subject."

Darian smiled. "No, not now. The music is nice. I just wish I'd have had a chance to listen to more of it." She turned toward him. "I like western swing."

"Do you like to dance?"

"Oh, gosh, no. I'm not much of a dancer. Too busy to socialize much."

Tom sighed. "I hear that." He laughed a little and shook his head as if remembering a private joke.

"What?"

"I was just thinking," he said and glanced at her, his eyes crinkled and rueful. "The hours you and I spent yesterday on horseback were the closest thing I've had to a date in . . . weeks. No, months."

Darian laughed. "Me, too. Gee, our first date. You sure know how to show a lady a good time."

"No flowers, no dinner, no dancing—just the thrill of the moonlight chase."

Darian grimaced. "The thrill of the morning after."

Their laughter faded, and the silence, along with unasked questions, hung between them. "Tom," Darian said. "I'm going to be very blunt and forward and ask you a personal question."

"Please do."

"You said you love having kids out at Clearpool?"

"Oh, yeah," he answered softly. He obviously knew what she was going to ask, so she didn't say it. She just waited.

"I guess you know I'm divorced. Yes? Well, we never had any kids." He shrugged. "Who knows? My marriage may have survived if we'd had a family, but I doubt it." He glanced over at her. "Annalea and I wanted children, but it just didn't work out. Probably for the best. We'd probably be fighting about where and how to raise them." He faced the road again. "We fought about everything else."

"I'm really sorry. I didn't mean to—"

"Not at all," he said. "It's only fair. After all, I know I asked a lot of personal questions about you and Joel. Besides, none of this is any secret. I was twenty-seven when I met Annalea at Mardi Gras. I was doing some work for my father and Southern Louisiana Energy. Anyway, we got married pretty fast, and everything was okay as long as we lived in New Orleans.

"She came from a huge Catholic family, six girls, five boys, and they were all really close. She wanted a big family, too, and that suited me fine. I hated being an only child. Eventually my job finished and we came back here. She wasn't too happy in Austin, but she made an effort to adjust. Then Tuffy got sick and passed away, and after that I had to take over everything—the ranch, the corporation—all of it. Annalea felt more and more isolated out here. No family. No culture or parties. Not enough attention from me. She left once it became obvious that my life wasn't going to change."

"Maybe it is best the two of you didn't have kids. There's always other chances. I mean if you get married again."

He looked over at her. "I can't have kids, Darian."

Real pain. Darian saw that she'd opened a very deep wound. "I... I'm sorry. I shouldn't—"

He shrugged. "It's okay. Don't look so upset. But it seems weird, doesn't it? Big, healthy guy like me. I had a fever when I was ten. That finished it for me, I just didn't know until after I was married."

"I've heard of things like this before. Aren't there procedures? I know there are laboratories that specialize in—"

"I know. For a while Annalea and I hoped...well, but it didn't work out. First the medicine made her really sick. And she was rather fragile. All those invasive procedures hurt too much. Scared her too bad."

"Are you really sure? I mean there're lots of—"

"Let me put it this way. I've undergone batteries of the most humiliating tests a man could ever take, and they all say that the likelihood of me fathering a child is roughly the same as rain falling on the moon."

"Tom, I'm sorry to bring up—"

"Ah, hush that. It's probably all for the best. As it is, the place is swarming with kids all the time anyway. Dominga's boys are like mine. There are at least twenty kids living on the place most of the year, so I get to indulge my fatherly instincts pretty thoroughly." He grinned. "And if they get too aggravating, I just send them back to their folks."

The uncomfortable moment didn't pass easily. Darian wanted to say something to move to a more pleasant subject, but everything she thought of seemed awkward and contrived—more likely to make things worse than better. She gazed out the window and listened to the tires humming on the blacktop, and murmured the words of the song.

At the Dripping Springs turnoff, Tom turned down the music. "Okay, now I get to ask you a personal question."

Darian laughed. "Go ahead."

"You said you don't socialize. Why?"

She lifted her hands in a gesture of helplessness. "Like I said, who's got time?" He raised a skeptical eyebrow at her. "Well, think about it. How could I possibly maintain another relationship in my life? I work at least ten hours a day and I have since I was in college. And if I do have an evening to spare, I almost always want to do something with Jason. He's fun to be with." She chuckled a little. "Well, most of the time. Anyway, I don't enjoy dating. That whole stupid getting-to-know-you scene. And suppose I found somebody I cared to be with? What would I do? How would I fit it in?"

Tom nodded. "I know exactly what you're saying." He paused. "So do you think you'll ever marry again?"

Darian sighed. "Funny, in some ways, I'd really like to be married. Jason needs it. I want to be part of a family, too, but I can't imagine it ever working out. I could never be the traditional stay-at-home wife. My commitments are just too demanding. And what about the time involved to get a relationship started? To maintain it—"

Once again his gaze cut toward her. "You know, that's exactly the problem I've got. I'd like to be married, but I don't have time to, you know, court someone. I've a ranch to run plus the rest of the businesses." He gripped the steering wheel. "That's what drove Annalea away. She needed more attention. I just couldn't give it to her."

He looked at her and grinned. "So what about romance, love and all that?"

Darian laughed. "Bah, humbug and...double humbug. I tried love, romance and all that once and it was a disaster. It was certainly nothing to build a marriage on."

Tom shrugged. "Most people do build their marriages on it, though."

Darian faced him. "Yes, and look how most marriages end."

"So what do you think a good marriage is built on?"

Darian paused. She'd done some thinking about this, but she'd never talked about it aloud. "Well, I think it should be a partnership of two people with complementary life goals. For me, anyway, it would have to be based on a similar outlook on life, understanding, respect and...friendship."

"Well, that's the way it used to be, isn't it? For hundreds of years, people would arrange marriages for lots of reasons—family, money, land—reasons that never included romance."

Darian turned toward the road. "I know it doesn't sound very romantic, but a marriage based on more stable and permanent elements would sure have a better

chance than one based on temporary hormonal or emotional..."

"Insanity?" Tom offered.

They both laughed.

By five o'clock that afternoon, Darian's shoulders and
neck were once again on fire with familiar pain. Richard
had been through four drafts already, and Darian
couldn't get her part completed because the client had
made some mistakes in filling out the questionnaire.

She was also feeling queasy due to too much coffee on
an empty stomach. The only food they could get delivered on Sunday was pizza, and although Darian cruised
the vending machines for something less volatile to her
tender middle, she couldn't find anything that looked
remotely edible.

"Damn," she muttered. "You'd have to be completely desperate to eat this stuff. None of this food is
even food. It's—it's cardboard held together with indus-
trial dye." She gave the machine a look of disgust and
made a cup of tea for dinner.

At five-thirty, after spending more than twenty hours
at the firm in two days, Richard buzzed her to say he'd
reached his limit and had decided to go home. On his way
out he stopped by Darian's office, looking disheveled in
old corduroys and a day-old beard. "I'm seeing double,
Dee. I'm going to go home and lapse into a nice coma for
a while. I know you said the flags from the auction are
supposed to be delivered later this week, but tell me one
more time what I'm supposed to say in case anybody asks
about yesterday."

Darian set her pencil down and rubbed her neck. "If
anyone says anything, just tell them Jason got lost, and

Tom and his friends helped us find him. I'm going to really play it down."

"Good idea. Neither of us'll ever make partner if Atwell gets stirred up."

Darian took off her glasses and rubbed her eyes. "No kidding. If anyone asks, dissemble your buns off."

Richard saluted. "Ten-four."

"Till tomorrow."

"Tomorrow."

When he left, she rested her forehead on her hands. All afternoon her concentration had been broken by thoughts of Jason and Tom. Now, sitting at her desk in her office, the whole experience seemed somehow dreamlike and unreal.

Her aches and pains were real though, just like the decisions she had to make. What about Jason and the dog? She grimaced as she sat back in her chair and pressed her hands against her spine.

Tom Steinbuck had been wonderful. Strong, kind, witty and generous. Nice-looking in a rugged, outdoorsy way. Much different than the urbane, sophisticated men she dealt with most of the time. There would never be any question about where you stood with a man like Tom. With litigators, everything was a constant negotiation. A never-ending battle of one-upmanship, subtle manipulation and probing for possible weakness, even in social situations.

Ranch life seemed much less complicated. Weather, livestock, land and water—all those things, though powerful elements, would present honest, straightforward challenges. Just like Tom.

Darian shook her head. *You're daydreaming. You don't have time for this.*

The phone rang then and she flinched. Jason was phoning early. Darian smiled ruefully. Her son would probably be as close to perfect as he could manage for the next few weeks. "Darian Conroy," she said.

"Darian?"

There was no mistaking the voice on the phone. The baritone had the same effect it had the first time she'd heard it—unseen fibers all along her spine rose as if attracted by some powerful magnetism. "Tom. I was just thinking of you."

"Must be my lucky day," he said. "Listen, it turned out that I'm the one who's bringing Jason home. As a matter of fact, I'm in my car and I've got Jason with me. We'll be in Austin in about thirty minutes, and I wondered if you'd let me take the two of you to dinner."

"Oh, Tom, I wish I would have known. Mrs. Steen is at the house and she's made a Sunday dinner. Pot roast, potatoes, the whole thing." She hesitated. "Would you like to join us instead? We'd love to have you."

"I'd love to. I accept."

Thirty minutes later, Darian greeted Tom and Jason at the front door. While her son tore through the house to show Winnie to Mrs. Steen, Darian took Tom's coat. Although Darian had always been proud of her home, which had been decorated by one of Austin's best designers, for the first time it seemed to be missing something. She attributed her lack of confidence to customary hostess nerves. After all, Tom had never seen her place. It was important that he like it.

During dinner, he effortlessly charmed Mrs. Steen and kept them all entertained with ranch stories. Jason was obviously in the throes of hero worship, and Mrs. Steen was flustered and blushed often as she fussed around him, dishing up enormous helpings of beef and potatoes. Darian realized it was the first time they'd ever had a man sitting at their table.

After dinner, Jason took Winnie for a walk, but was sent up to bed immediately after. Darian and Tom sat talking over coffee in her living room.

"Mrs. Steen will probably quit," Darian said ruefully. "I didn't mention Winnie to her before you brought Jason home. She hates animals." Darian set her mug down on the marble-topped coffee table. "I feel sorry for the puppy, too, but I really shouldn't keep her. It would be like rewarding Jason for stealing. And look at this place. There's no yard to speak of. And Jason's involved in school and sports. How could we take care of a puppy?"

Tom glanced at the mug in his hands. "I don't know. But like I heard a lady say once, little boys just naturally love puppies."

"True."

"Why don't I keep her at Clearpool? Just until you decide what you want to do, I mean."

"Thanks for offering, Tom. Once again you've come to my rescue." Darian sat back in her chair. So strange, she thought, to see a man sitting on her china-print sofa, long legs stretched out, large hands around one of her little cups. "How many times are you going to save me before you get tired of it?"

He smiled. "It's my pleasure."

At that moment she decided. "Well, I think I'll accept your offer about the puppy. At least until I can decide what to do permanently. And about Jason, I think it would be good for him. If you're sure it's not too much trouble."

He studied her through dark blue eyes. "Of course, I'm sure."

When they finished their coffee, Darian went upstairs to tell Jason what had been decided. She brought Winnie down, and the puppy curled up on the front seat of Tom's four-wheel drive. Darian stood by his door while he threw his coat into the back seat. He really is tall, she thought.

"Well, goodbye, again," she said. "Like I said, I'll drive Jason up on Friday."

"But we'll talk before then, I'm sure."

"Oh, of course." She looked up at him. His face was very close to hers, and she could see that he was studying her. His eyes roamed her face as if searching for something.

Once again, unseen fibers sprang to life, urging her toward him. Darian tilted her head up slightly. *You're playing with fire. Oh, don't be stupid. He just wants to kiss good-night. It's only polite. I'm his hostess.*

As soon as her head tilted back, Tom's lips parted slightly, and he moved toward her. Darian knew he'd received the sign he was waiting for, and he slipped his arm around her. She remembered how it felt to be held in those arms. Against that broad chest. Just one little kiss. No big thing.

As soon as his lips touched hers, she sighed. It was as if he'd kissed her a thousand times before. His hands, his warm mouth, everything molded perfectly against her. His lips, his gentle tongue, the almost-unheard rumble in his chest—everything was as if he knew exactly what she liked. What she needed. His flat stomach pressed against hers, and she felt her heart beating against his chest.

I've been starving, she thought. I didn't even know I was hungry.

When the kiss ended, Darian stepped back and looked down. "Uh, I . . . uh—"

"I know. Me, too."

She looked up and smiled a little ruefully, wanting to smooth the moment with humor. "We should both get out more."

He grinned and they laughed quietly. "Forget that. No one would have us. Actually, we should get married," he said. "We're perfect for each other."

"Good idea. We should do it just to see the expressions on our friends' faces."

She began to back up, distancing herself. "Thanks again for everything. I'll talk to you later."

He raised his hand and she stood and watched until he began to back up. What a pleasant evening, she told herself. Maybe this business with Jason will turn out to be the best thing. Tom Steinbuck would be a wonderful, if brief, influence in his life—a fine man with decent, uncorrupted morals and no hidden agenda.

And a great kisser.

She shook her head. No point in thinking about that. She was glad she and Tom had discussed their life-styles on the way home from Clearpool. He would never expect anything personal to develop between them. Of all people in the world, Tom Steinbuck knew how pointless it would be to even consider such a thing.

Darian switched off the light in the foyer. The house was quiet, settled into itself for the night, but just before she locked the door and set the alarm, Darian paused listening. For the briefest instant, she thought she'd heard an unfamiliar sound.

A distant warning clang.

Chapter Five

"Good morning, Darian. Wow, what a pretty dress."

"Well, thank you, Marty. I'm glad you like it." Since she wouldn't be in court that day, Darian wore a simple Lillian Kelly sweater-dress of pink cashmere. The soft wool nuzzled luxuriously against her skin and made a delightful, feminine change from weeks of being bound into somber, sincere-looking suits and sensible pumps.

"Congratulations on Brookwood."

Darian smiled. "Thanks. We had a good jury."

"We had a good *lawyer*."

"Well, thank you for saying so, but don't give me too much credit. I was just one of the team."

Marty made a face and handed Darian her messages. "Oh, you're just too modest. I heard your closing argument was brilliant."

Darian dropped her eyelids and struck a brief pose. "Well, this is true."

"Besides all those calls, Tom Steinbuck phoned twice, but he didn't leave a number. He said he was out running around and he'd have to call you back."

Darian set her briefcase down. "Did he say what he wanted?"

Marty made a dramatic pause and gave Darian a why-didn't-you-tell-me look. "He said to just say your future husband called and was frantically looking for you."

Darian took one look at the expression on her secretary's face and gave a snorting laugh. "Oh, Marty, for Pete's sake. It's a running private joke. You know? A joke. Ha ha. Since both of us are so hopeless, we just kid that we're going to have to get married since no one else would have either of us."

"Oh, a joke. Ha ha." Marty looked crestfallen but skeptical. "Too bad. He sounds cute."

"Actually, he's gorgeous, and I wish I did have somebody to fix him up with. But like I said, he wouldn't have time for anyone anyway."

"Oh. Okay. How's Jason doing?"

For the first time in months, Darian could smile when someone asked her that question. "He's a different kid. He's so happy and his grades are back up. I had no idea that just spending the weekends with...I mean I just wish I would have known earlier what a difference being at the ranch would make. He can drive a tractor and he's learning to ride. Tom's been really busy, but he's taken Jason and some other boys camping and fishing and hunting for arrowheads."

"How long's he been going out there now?"

"This will be the fourth weekend. Actually, I'm staying over when I drive him up this Friday. Since we're not in trial I have a little time, and Jason's been begging me to come up."

"Good. You need it."

She picked up her briefcase. "Maybe so. Well, I better go start on these calls. Remind me to tell you what they did to poor Clyde for Halloween."

"Who's Clyde?"

Before Darian could answer, the phone rang. A double ring.

"Darian Conroy's office. This is Marty, can I—oh, hi." She put the call on hold and gave Darian a knowing smile. "It's your future husband."

Darian rolled her eyes and headed for her office. Once inside, she picked up the phone.

"Hi, Tom."

"Hello, counselor. I hope I didn't call at a bad time."

"Well, I do have the Joint Chiefs on the other line," Darian paused for a dramatic moment. "But since it's you they can wait."

Tom chuckled. "I'm glad to see you have your priorities straight. Now if that was the partnership com—"

"Don't even joke about that. Only four more months. I'm going to chew my nails down to the second knuckle."

"I'm sure you don't have a thing to worry about. With your record and the hours you put in, they'd be nuts not to make you partner."

"From your lips to God's ear. By the way, thanks again for the flowers and the wine. Purple irises are my favorites, and I'm going to save that merlot until you can enjoy it with me."

"Deal. But I just wish I would have known about your birthday in advance. Jason didn't tell me until the weekend after."

Darian sighed melodramatically. "Well, from now on I'll make sure you get a shopping day countdown, just like Christmas. As of today, you only have three hundred fifty-five shopping days left. Or better yet, why not just send me your platinum card and I'll take care of that pesky shopping for you."

His laughter, booming and masculine, was infectious, and Darian found herself laughing along with him.

"You know," he said. "I just might do that." There was a sly pause. "If I could get you to do the rest of my shopping for me."

"No way. I hate shopping."

"Me, too," he said. "Once again, Darian, we're just alike."

Silence stretched out between them, and Darian felt there was something expected of her, but she didn't quite know what. "Did you call for some special reason, or just to give my secretary something to gossip about?"

"You know after I hung up I was worried that she might take my joke seriously, but then I thought, oh, hell, surely she could tell I was only kidding."

"Well, I told her it was a joke, but I got the feeling there's going to be a fresh rumor grinding in the rumor mill."

"Great publicity for me," he said. Then his voice grew serious. "But really, Darian, I wouldn't want to do anything to cause you embarrassment. I was just being exuberant and stupid and I—"

"Oh, don't worry about it. Like I said, I told her it was just a joke. Besides, that kind of rumor would only do me good." Darian twisted the cord and rocked back in her chair. "In fact, the firm would be thrilled if I got married. They don't like loose ends, and nothing makes them more nervous than divorced or single associates."

"Well," Tom began slowly, "since I've lulled you with flowers, wine and the possibility of marriage, I wonder if I can talk you into doing me a favor?"

"If I can, I'd be happy to. What is it?"

He sighed heavily. "You're gonna hate this, but there's a cocktail party and reception at Crocket Mansion Thursday night. A couple of years ago the ranch donated some property to the university and now there's a dedication ceremony. Somebody or other commissioned a bronze of Tuffy, and I have to go be gracious and jerk the sheet off of it. Daphne—my mother—was supposed to represent the family, but she's gone down with some bug. Anyway, I was wondering if you'd come as my guest. It's black tie, but I promise it won't drag on too long."

"I'd be delighted. And Thursday's good for me. Since the trial is over, I've got a little breathing room for a couple of weeks."

"Great. I'll pick you up at six-thirty."

"Fine. I'll look forward to it."

When he hung up, Darian sat motionless. When the buzz of the dial tone suddenly erupted into the angry beeping of an unreplaced receiver, she shook her head and set the phone down in its cradle. Odd, she thought, that she should drift away into reverie like that. *That's weird. Since when am I uptight about what I wear? I'll wear something and I'll look fine. I always look appropriate.*

Appropriate? But I want to look more than appropriate. I want to look dazzling. Get a grip, Darian. No one will even notice you. If anyone does notice what you look like, it's only because you'll be hanging on the guest of honor's arm. Besides, you're smart and that's better than being pretty. Now, clear your head and read your mail. You wasted the whole day yesterday glad-handing with everybody about the trial. You'll never make partner staring out the window and having clothing fantasies.

By eleven she had dictated answers to the day's correspondence, written a closing memo to her section leader regarding Brookwood, and calculated her billable hours for the case. She was just drafting her part of the proposed final judgment when Marty buzzed a call through.

"Marty, I'm going nuts in here. Would you mind telling—"

"It's Mr. Huntingdon."

"Oh. Thanks." She sat up straight in her chair as if he could somehow see through the phone. "Hello. This is Darian."

"Darian. Atwell here. Could you join a meeting in the large conference room on twelve, please."

"Of course. I'll be right there." Darian's heart began to beat slightly faster. She liked the feeling, though. It reminded her of the way she used to feel just before the starter's gun fired and she hit the water, stroking powerfully, knowing she was totally prepared and very, very good at what she did.

When she walked into the conference room, it took an act of will to smile graciously. They were all there, Endor Thorogood, admiral of the fleet of the firm's deadliest litigators. A former state Supreme Court judge and senior partner, he was tall, slightly stooped and had a kindly, professorial air that often caused the inexperienced to underestimate his ruthlessness. He was flanked by Irvin Banes, Scott Kyle and the rest of the senior partners in the trial section.

Richard and four other associates sat scattered around the room, and apparently the discussion was well under way because none of them so much as glanced at her. Darian didn't see any open files on the long oval table, but everyone else had brought a legal pad just as she did.

She took the closest empty chair, sat down and tried to catch up.

"Oh, Darian, here you are," Atwell said, as if she'd just materialized. "Please consider this a completely confidential briefing. Tomorrow morning's papers are going to be screaming with headlines that Goldenair has filed an antitrust suit against Consolidated Skyway. This will be, not counting the Four Corners Nuclear Power Plant, of course," he said, nodding deferentially toward Judge Thorogood, "the most significant litigation the firm has ever been engaged in. Since you've proven so adept at discovery, you'll be working on Endor's team. We'll try to clear the rest of your docket, of course. Now, ladies and gentlemen, this is what we know so far...."

Forty-five minutes later, Darian left the conference room with Richard. "This is it, Dee," he said. His voice revealed the same tension and excitement she was feeling. "If we do this right, we're in."

"I know," she said. Her partnership was close enough to see. Close enough to taste. The culmination of years and years of grinding study, sacrifice and work. For years, she hadn't allowed herself to look beyond the goal of partnership. Now that it was attainable, she could almost allow herself a glimpse of life beyond being an associate.

Having proven herself to her firm, and then to the legal community at large, she would be a more viable advocate; she would be able to choose her cases and how she spent her considerable energy but limited time. And then there was the prestige and financial rewards.

Still, there would be a subtle increase in other pressures. Life at the top often made you an easier target, but that was okay, too. Darian knew her work would stand up to scrutiny anytime.

"You want to have lunch, Dee?" Richard said. "I'm going to Pippin's."

"No, thanks, Rich," she said thoughtfully. "I've got some stuff to clear up, so I'm having lunch at my desk. Thanks, though." On her way back to her office, she stopped at the vending machine for cheese crackers and a bag of chips.

Thursday evening at six-twenty, Darian's doorbell rang. "I'll get that, Mrs. Steen. It's bound to be Mr. Steinbuck."

When she opened the door, she stood dumbfounded for a moment. For the first time, she saw Tom Steinbuck dressed in something other than jeans, and the effect was slightly startling.

He was dressed formally, and the black tailored fabric sat square and elegant on his broad shoulders and dropped in acute angles to his narrow hips. The brilliant starched shirt made his tanned skin look even darker, his eyes more smoky blue.

"Tom," she said. "You... you—come in."

He didn't move for a moment, but stood staring at her as if dumbfounded. "What?"

"Would... would you like to come in?"

"Oh, yes. Of course. Sorry." He shook his head as if annoyed with himself as he entered the foyer. "I'm sorry, Darian. I just never... I mean, you look gorgeous. Stunning, in fact."

"Why, thank you," she said. "You're looking resplendent yourself."

"You like it?" He held his arms away from his body and looked down at himself. "It's new. I always feel a little ridiculous in a monkey suit."

"On the contrary, you should dress in black tie more often. I've never seen you looking so wonderful."

"Well, thanks for saying so, but you—" He took her hands, lifted them and stepped away. "Now *you* should be going somewhere special, not just one of these tea-cake-and-kissy-face things. You look dazzling."

Dazzling. Darian felt the beginnings of a pleasant flush. She knew she looked her best. She had bought the dress a year earlier without knowing if she'd ever have a chance to wear it. But at the time, it was simply too wonderful to pass up—an armless sheath of royal blue silk that hugged her body from bust to ankle except for the slit that revealed a scandalous stretch of leg and thigh.

The dress accentuated her best features—classic shoulders, shapely arms and marvelous unfreckled skin—a gift from some distant tinge of Mediterranean blood. Although the adequate bustline she once had was sadly depleted after Jason's birth, she still had her flat stomach, and despite her lack of time to exercise, her long legs were still firm and slim.

To show off her grandmother's tiny sapphire earrings, she wore her thick hair loosely piled on her head in a Gibson Girl bun and let long wisps trail down around her face and neck, while around her neck, she'd fastened the diamond drop her mother gave her as a law-school graduation present. But best of all, she knew she wore the glow that comes from happiness in general and wearing beautiful, new clothes.

"Thank you for saying so."

"No, thank you. Every man there is going to want to club me in the head."

His eyes crinkled when he smiled, and Darian noticed again how white his teeth were. Not perfect, but big and square and strong-looking. "Would you like a drink, or do we need to go?"

He pulled his sleeve back. "Actually, we'd probably better fly."

At that moment, there was a low thunder of footsteps on the stairs and Jason appeared on the landing, eyes alight. "Tom!" He flew down the remainder of the steps and flung himself past Darian and into the man's arms.

Tom hugged him roughly and tousled his hair. "Hey, buddy. Good to see you. Lookin' forward to this weekend?"

"Yeah, so's Tony. I told him about Clyde, but he doesn't believe he's that big."

"He'll see."

"Yeah, he'll see." He turned toward his mother. "Wow, mom. You look cool." He elbowed Tom. "What a babe, huh?"

Darian rolled her eyes. "Jason Conroy, I'm your mother. And what do you mean 'babe'? Who talks like that?"

Two pair of male eyes steadfastly refused to meet hers. "I'll get my wrap," she said.

The drive from Darian's town house to Crocket Mansion took less than twenty minutes. A slow-moving line of cars filed through the oak-lined circular drive of the mansion, and Darian was slightly surprised to see so many vehicles. "How many people will be here?"

He sighed. "Too many. I guess a couple of hundred."

"*What?*"

"Oh, yeah. There's always a big turnout for these university soirees. There'll definitely be some people from your firm. Marva Wallace and David Thale represent us on energy matters, and I know I've worked with at least half the guys in your trusts department. Of course Atwell and his wife'll be there. He's a regent at the school.''

Darian's earlier enthusiasm paled slightly. She should have known there would be people from the firm. Sternwell was the oldest and largest law firm in Texas, and the partners were involved in every level of society—education, politics, industry. But why did it have to be Atwell? Just when she thought she might have one relaxed evening enjoying herself with a handsome, interesting friend.

Guests filled the foyer and receiving room of the mansion, and as soon as Darian and Tom walked in, an unmistakable flutter of interest rippled through the elegant little groups. Darian immediately saw Atwell and his wife speaking with one of the district judges.

If Atwell Huntingdon was a shark, his wife, Lorelei, was a dolphin—round, ebullient and effusively friendly. She gave a little scream of delight as soon as she saw them, and surged across the foyer brandishing a half-empty champagne glass.

"Darian. Tom. How marvelous to see you both. What an incredible dress, my dear. How've you been?"

"Just fi—"

Lorelei looped her arm through Darian's and dragged her a step or two away to ask in a conspiratorial but nonetheless reverberating whisper, "What's this very interesting rumor I hear about you and that handsome fellow there? I understand we may be hearing wedding bells soon."

"Good heavens, Lorelei. Who told you that?"

The little woman tipped her head to one side giving Darian the benefit of a broad stage wink. "Oh, just a little birdie. And isn't it all too wonderful? Just because Atwell sent you in his place to that auction. I think it's just about the most romantic thing I've ever heard. Do you have any definite plans, dear? You know I wouldn't tell a soul."

I plan to murder my secretary first thing tomorrow morning.

"Lorelei," Tom said evenly. "How wonderful to see you again." With a gracious handshake, he pried Darian loose and steered her deeper into the crowd.

The rest of the evening was a pleasant blur of conversation, admiring glances, champagne and cordial curiosity. No one questioned them as bluntly as Lorelei Huntingdon, but there was no mistaking the inquisitive stares and sudden whispers every time Tom and Darian appeared. After the bronze—a rugged, magnificent bust by Mercedes Tane—was unveiled, Tom and Darian politely thanked their hosts and fled.

Once settled safely back in the car, Tom took her hand. "Darian, thank you so much for being such a good sport. I had no idea—"

"Oh, it's okay." She sighed and squeezed his hand in a friendly, reassuring way. "Like my mother says, 'When they're talking about you, they're thinking about you.'"

"Well, thanks be to your mom for being so smart and rescuing me."

They drove in silence for a few minutes, but Tom moved restlessly in his seat. Darian could tell he was glancing at her from the corner of his eye, but she thought she'd wait until he decided to say what was bothering him.

"Darian?"

"Mmm?"

"Do you have plans for Thanksgiving?"

She sighed. "It's my year to have my mother. I have two sisters. Bea edits *Businesswoman* in New York, and Johanna is an orthopedic surgeon in San Diego. Since we're so spread out, my mother spends Thanksgiving with one of us each year and then, for Christmas, everybody is supposed to go to her house in Dallas."

"Do you think she'd like to come out to Clearpool? It's a stampede." He glanced over at her and smiled. "But a really friendly stampede. My mother always comes, but she's been so sick this year, she may not travel. There's always lots of food and friends and kids of friends. I'm pretty sure Jason'd like it."

"Thanks for inviting us. I think I'd like that, but I need to check with Mother, of course."

Darian thought about his offer. What would Paulina Sedgewick say if her youngest daughter brought her to Clearpool Ranch for Thanksgiving? It would certainly be a break from their traditional holiday dinner—always so quiet, two single women and a bored little boy picking at food he really didn't like that much. Who knows? Maybe Paulina would enjoy herself, but it was always so hard to tell.

They arrived back at Darian's a little after eleven. The house was dark and quiet. Mrs. Steen slept upstairs in the room across from Jason's, and the light on the landing was turned low and warmed the stairs with soft semi-darkness.

"Would you like a cup of coffee?"

"I'd love one, but are you sure it's not too late?"

"Well, not for me. I don't need much sleep. Ever since law school I never sleep more than a few hours. But I don't want to put you on the road too late."

"It's not too late for me, but I don't want to put you to too much trouble."

"Oh, for Pete's sake, listen to us. We sound like those little overly polite cartoon chipmunks. Why don't I just make instant?"

His laugh was quiet and deep in his throat. "Deal."

They spoke in whispers, and when they reached the kitchen, Darian didn't turn on the overhead light, but flipped on the little table lamp. She was in a comfortable, slightly dreamy state, and bright lights or loud voices seemed an unpleasant intrusion.

Tom leaned against the counter while she moved quietly about the kitchen. She filled the electric kettle, took out two mugs, the coffee and spoons. Over the stove, the silly cat clock slowly moved its tail left, then right while his round, watchful eyes turned in counterpoint. Left. Right. Tick. Tock.

She didn't move to sit down in a chair, but stood by Tom. For some reason she was afraid to look directly into his eyes. *I'm just feeling shy because I've never had a man in here this late.* But the truth was she felt something happening. Something subtle but profound. An expectancy vibrated in the air around her, and she began to feel slightly ill at ease.

The kettle began a quiet rumble as the element heated up. Darian shifted from one foot to the other and tried to think of something to say, but the silence had stretched tight like the tension holding water in an overfilled glass. If she said the wrong thing, something would spill over. Make a mess. Spoil things.

She wanted to unstrap her sandals or unpin her hair. Something. The clasp of the necklace felt as if it had tangled in her hair, and she reached up and tried to undo it.

"Let me," Tom murmured, and faced her, standing close. His hands slid beneath hers, over the bare skin of her shoulders, and met behind her neck. His hands were large and warm, but Darian shivered when she felt his fingers touching her nape, the place just where her hair grew thin and wispy. The kettle boiled, and a cloud of vapor gathered over the stove. Tom's fingers reached the clasp, but instead of unfastening it he began to pull the pins out of her hair and massage the heavy strands loose.

Darian felt his breath, the suggestion of his mouth, against her temple. She tilted her head to the side to let the sensation touch her eyelids. Then her cheek. Her lips.

His hands flattened against the bare skin of her back as he gathered her to himself. She knew what would happen. She remembered from the first time. And her lips remembered. And her hands, and the throbbing awareness that shot down between her breasts and insisted that she press her body against his....

His mouth slanted back and forth over hers, hungry one moment, soothing the next, but always urging her to a higher, deeper intensity. She could feel her heart banging against him. Or was it his? He turned and pressed her against the counter, and all along the length of him, she could feel the acceleration of his muscular power—the intensifying animal masculinity in him. She knew if she allowed herself, if she would just let her awareness seek what it wanted—to press here and here, there would be the awakening of a deeper, more elemental arousal.

For one moment she almost gave in; the torture of approaching that brink was sweet in itself. It felt so good. It had been so long, but the force of her own desire demanded that she make a decision. She took her mouth from him, but groaned aloud as she did. "Tom. Wait. I can't. I..."

He groaned, too. "I know. I know."

He held her for long moments while the banging of their hearts slowed. She listened to her breath slowing down. To his. The water in the kettle bubbled into silence, shut off by the built-in safety mechanism.

"I'm sorry, but I—"

"Shhh," he said. "I'm sorry."

"No, listen." She stepped away, and had to reach up to shove the hair back from her face. "You don't know how tempted I am—"

"Don't I?" he said, and winced slightly. "I think I do."

"But I can't do this, you see? If I...if we—"

"Don't say another word, Darian. I understand. I agree. We'd ruin our friendship and I'd hate that."

She looked up at him in wonder and gratitude. "You would?"

"Of course I would. I mean, I'm not saying that I wouldn't—I mean, what man in his right mind wouldn't want to... What I mean is, what we have—you, me and Jason—it's too important to me to mess up for any reason."

"Thank you."

"No. Thank you. Well, I think I'm going to take a rain check on the coffee. You're staying over with us on Friday, right? Good. I'll see you then. Thanks again for tonight. I'm the envy of every man in Austin."

She walked him to the door, but they didn't even touch hands again. Darian knew they'd come to a crossroads, an understanding. She told herself she had no regrets. Well, very few.

Everyone knows that sex ruined friendships, she told herself. I'm really glad we've gotten past this. From now on, I'll just have to be smart and careful, and avoid situations where he—either of us—might be tempted. After all, we're only human.

Thanksgiving at Clearpool was sounding more and more like a good idea. Time to start new traditions. Give Jason some new memories. And her mother would enjoy something new. She just knew it.

Chapter Six

"Well, I can't say I enjoyed Thanksgiving, Mr. Steinbuck, but it was certainly unique."

"I appreciate your honesty, Mrs. Sedgewick. Two spades down. Heart up. All this formality is getting to me. May I call you Paulina?"

"Yes, you may... Tom," she replied, her attention riveted to the cards she held.

It was well past midnight on the Friday after Thanksgiving, and Tom sat in his library with Paulina Sedgewick, dealing her another hand of Sergeant Major. They were in the third game of their sudden-death play-off for house champion and had been playing alone for hours. In the beginning all of Tom's house guests participated enthusiastically, except Darian who never played cards, but by Wednesday evening the others had become discouraged, and by Thanksgiving Day, no one else would play with either of them.

She tallied their current bids on the pad beside her. "Three diamonds up. Two clubs up."

"What part did you not enjoy? Dealer takes two this hand, knocks here." He eyed Paulina over his cards. Thin and tough as a stick with steel-colored hair and eyes to match, she radiated compressed energy and piercing intellect unsoftened by any hint of patience.

From the moment he'd seen her step out of Darian's car, he knew she was going to be a challenging house guest, and sure enough, within moments she had demonstrated both the range and sting of her bullwhip tongue. By the end of the day, all Tom's employees treated her as gingerly as an unexploded bomb. Rudy, in particular, after carrying her luggage into the house, disappeared into the barn and hadn't been seen since.

"Well, I suppose the same things that made it unique and interesting also utterly destroyed the traditional holiday atmosphere—the hot tamales for one thing. *Cabrito* and mariachis. Fireworks and all those blasted screaming children whacking away at that piñata. It's just not quite the way I visualize the Pilgrim forefathers giving thanks."

Tom listened for a moment to the quiet snap of the cards against the table and the soft rattle of ice drowning in his Scotch. "Well, my understanding of the Thanksgiving tradition is giving thanks *for* what you have *with* what you have. I believe the traditional foods the Pilgrims ate were just what was available to them and so, in that sense, I believe our Thanksgiving here is the most traditional one I know of. Besides," he said, totally unintimidated by her. "We had turkey and dressing, too."

"Fire in the hole," Paulina said, laying down four hearts, ace high.

Tom raised his eyebrows slightly at the recklessness of her move. Even for Paulina, a bid of one-fifty was extravagant. They played in silence for a few moments, and Tom laid each set of his books in a crisscross pattern. He knew Darian's mother had been building up to something for the past couple of days, but he had no intention of making it easy for her. She certainly hadn't made things easy for any of them. Especially Darian.

She cleared her throat. "My grandson really seems to be taken with you. From the moment he and Darian picked me up at the airport, your name was all I heard. It was 'Tom this' and 'Tom that.'"

Here we go. "Well, I'm flattered to hear that. Jason is the most remarkable boy I've ever known. It's been a pleasure to have him at Clearpool."

She tilted her head back to look at him through the bottom pane of her trifocals, her eyes bright and hard. "I understand this is the last weekend he'll be coming up here."

"I hope that's not true, but Darian tells me he's going to be more involved with his school activities for a while."

She smiled—a knowing, crafty smile. "That's very discreet of you, but I've heard about Jason's troubles at Fullingham. And what he did up here. And how you've been letting him work here to pay for the damage. Two spades up. Club down. I know all about it."

He tilted his head to the side. "Do you?"

"Yes. Although Darian didn't take me into her confidence, her older sister, Johanna, did after Darian saw fit to share it with her. I knew something was wrong with Darian. I could tell by her voice. You see, of my three daughters, she is the most like me."

Tom didn't answer aloud, but raised a skeptical eyebrow.

If Paulina was the least bit insulted, she didn't let it show. "Neither Johanna nor Beatrice ever suffered from the kind of sentimental notions that caused Darian so much trouble, but she *was* the youngest. And her father did dote on her. While he was with us, that is."

"She told me her dad died when she was ten. I'm sorry, that must have been hard for you."

Paulina smiled humorlessly. "But I don't suppose she told you he abandoned us when she was four. No? I thought not. Darian has a streak of blind loyalty that far exceeds good sense."

For one instant Tom caught a glimpse of Darian's mother as she might have been—a young, slender woman with three little girls and an absentee husband. Terrified by his abandonment and disillusioned in general, she would protect her children any way she could, and if that meant relentlessly driving them to become overachievers, well, so much the better.

"Darian paid a high price for her romantic fantasies, but she's long since gotten rid of that sort of foolishness. She adored her father, you know. I believe that's what attracted her to Joel. He was like Don. Diamond up. One heart down. She's also stubborn. Once she gets some notion in her head that things are a certain way, well—she'll cling to that notion despite clear evidence to the contrary." Her thin mouth flattened into the semblance of a smile. "But of course, she'd deny it.

"And has she told you about all the work she does for indigent women? Well, you should ask her to sometime." Paulina paused and studied her cards and the two piles on the table—her glance cutting from one to the other. "She's compelled to do community work because she feels the one who has the power is the one who has the responsibility. Don't you agree?''

"I'm sorry, Paulina, but I don't. I believe the one who has the responsibility is the one who has the responsibility. All men should be compelled to do their duty toward their children."

"That's very well for you," she said. "You came from a family who loved and protected you and provided for your security. There are many, many people—mostly women and children, I'm afraid—who are not given that luxury. That is why those of us who can must do whatever possible to protect those in our charge. I couldn't give my daughters money, but I could exhort them to apply themselves, to be responsible and independent and exploit all their talents to their fullest. I could warn them how stupid and destructive the wrong kind of attachments could be."

She took a sip of her tea, and Tom thought he could see a sheen in her silvery eyes. "And how utterly unforgivable it is to waste one's abilities. Of course, Darian's own experiences have taught her those lessons. Although her personal life has been somewhat of a disaster, her professional accomplishments are impressive, don't you think?"

Tom smiled. "Yes I do. Sergeant Major." He laid out his winning hand, letting each card smack against the table with its own satisfying little slap.

Paulina eyed the cards, took a prim breath and pursed her lips, then pulled her glasses off and let them fall on their chain against her flat chest. Without speaking, she reached down for her purse, opened her wallet and laid a five-dollar bill on the table. Tom didn't pick it up immediately, but smiled broadly, took a hefty swig from his glass, and crunched the ice. Nice and loud.

Paulina stood. "Well, I'm off to bed. It's much too late for me." She stood and smoothed her fine gray wool skirt down with one bony, spotted hand. "That is if I can ever manage to fall asleep, since I'm sure you've given me the lumpiest bed and the coldest room in this drafty old barn of a house."

"I'm glad you like it," Tom said, chuckling.

"Good night, Tom," she said. "No, don't get up." As she turned away she said, "I must say this is the most enjoyable game of Sergeant Major I've ever played."

Tom was certain Paulina would appreciate being goaded like the worthy adversary she'd proved herself to be. "But you lost," he said. Even though she couldn't actually see him gloat, he knew she'd hear it in his voice.

She turned her head just enough to show her face in profile. "Did I?"

As he watched her walk out of the room and down the hallway, his smile didn't fade. "So, Darian," he said quietly to himself. "That's what happened. Now I'm beginning to understand."

By Sunday afternoon Tom's other guests had departed for their homes, leaving only Darian, Paulina and Jason. It was just after three o'clock and Darian was sitting by herself on the front porch swing, moving it slowly with her toe. The bright November sun had warmed the temperature to the high, comfortable sixties, and Winnie was asleep in the yard—flat out on her side, paws and nose twitching. Jason and Eddie Villareal had gone off on horseback to Clearpool Source to try some fishing and they weren't expected back until four, and Paulina was in her room napping off another huge lunch. That left Darian deliciously alone to enjoy one last glass of wine before she faced the inevitable unpleasantness of packing up to go home.

Behind her the screen door creaked open. Booted feet thumped across the porch, and the old wicker chair behind her groaned when a familiar weight settled down. She didn't have to look. "Of all the wonderful meals this weekend, I think I enjoyed this lunch the most."

"It was good, wasn't it? I love Dominga's turkey almandine. She's packing you and Jason some stuff to take back. It looks like she plans on you feeding the five thousand. Or maybe she's afraid you don't eat enough."

Darian groaned. "Don't be ridiculous. You saw me. I hurt myself three days in a row." She sighed in contentment. High in the oak tree that spread its possessive arms over the porch, an unseen bird burst into a throbbing song. Paused. Warbled another emotional, heartrending aria. "What is that?"

"Mockingbird."

She turned slightly to see him. That familiar face—strong jaw, ruddy skin and happy eyes. His thick, dark hair was ruined as usual by the crease from his hat. "You want to join me on this swing?"

He grinned. "I thought you'd never ask."

She sat up and swung her legs down.

"Don't do that," he said quietly. "I'll feel guilty about making you move. Here, just lean against me."

She smiled and turned around and then settled against him, her back pressed against his strong, round shoulder. "I'm not smushing you, am I?"

"You're fine," he rumbled.

"Good. You feel comfy." The vibration of his voice against her back raised a tickle that teased through her body and sent little flutters along her torso.

"What time do you have to go back?"

"Paulina's plane leaves at seven, so we shouldn't leave later than five. There may be traffic."

"Oh, yeah. Of course."

Somewhere beyond the barn, a calf bawled for its mother, and in moments her exasperated answer boomed across the pasture. Darian smiled. The smells and sounds and sights were so different here. Sparrows bouncing on the dry ground in search of crumbs, then stopping for gleeful, frantic dust baths. The quiet at night and the sharp smell of pine and bruised cedar.

"I'm going to miss driving up here. I know Jason will, too. Not to mention Winnie. I hope she adjusts to life in town."

Darian was wearing an old cable-knit sweater Tom had lent her, and he picked at one of the fuzz balls on her arm. "And I'm going to miss all of you, too. Having Jason here has really filled up a place I didn't even know was empty. I can't tell you how much fun it's been teaching him to ride and shoot, and showing him the ranch. It's like I'm getting to be a kid again—you know, experiencing all those things all for the first time."

He sighed and his voice became more quiet. Pensive. "A few weeks ago, when this started, I was congratulating myself about what a great guy I was. I didn't realize how much I was going to get out of the deal myself."

There was nothing for Darian to say. Of course Tom had grown attached to Jason. Who wouldn't? He was the most wonderful little boy in the world. How many times at school plays had she shaken her head and wondered how the other parents could stand it—seeing their ordinary children so overwhelmingly outshone by her son. She smiled to herself then, admitting there probably wasn't a mother on earth who didn't feel exactly the same way. A quick scan of the auditorium had always revealed glowing faces and chests as swollen with pride as hers.

But at the same time she didn't feel sorry for Tom and knew he hadn't meant for her to. But still, it seemed a shame—a man like Tom would be an excellent father, and living at Clearpool would be any child's fantasy. "I'm surprised you've never done anything like this before. Have boys like Jason up here, I mean."

"Never had time I guess. Taking over for Tuffy was a nightmare. I never realized how much the old man did. He used to always joke that he taught me everything I knew—not everything *he* knew. I found out the hard way that he wasn't really kidding. And after I got the corporation under control, the oil market went nuts again. Then we had the worst drought in the history of the hill country. You know, always something."

Darian murmured a quiet assent. Something unexpected and complicated always seemed to throw itself directly across the path of a well-planned life. She checked her watch and heaved an enormous sigh. "Well, I better go and start gathering our stuff." She swung her legs down and looked Tom in the face. "Maybe later on when things settle down for all of us we can come back for another long weekend. I've enjoyed our talks so much."

Tom nodded, but his smile didn't touch his eyes. "I'd really like that, but from what you say, this airline thing you're working on isn't going to do anything but get more demanding for months, right?"

"I'm afraid so. I've already got fifty file boxes full of exhibits to go through in the next four months. Not counting my other cases. And then I have to start whatever discovery they want me to do. It's going to be nuts."

"Any idea when this thing will go to trial?"

Darian shook her head. "Since it's so huge and there are some really far-reaching antitrust implications, I give it at least thirty-six months, maybe more. In the meantime, I'm supposed to try to clear the rest of my docket."

"Well," Tom said. "Maybe at spring break you can come out." He stood and reached out a hand to help her up. "In the meantime, I'll call you if I make it to town. Maybe Mrs. Steen will have me over for dinner."

"We'd like that."

"Mom, why do you keep doing that?" Jason asked peevishly.

"Doing what?"

"You keep rubbing your neck, and wagging your head back and forth, back and forth. Like this."

"Well, my neck hurts. Do you mind?" She was snapping at him. She didn't mean to. "It always hurts," she added quietly. She knew he was disappointed about leaving the ranch. He had stared out the back window long after the ranch had disappeared. Still, nothing excused his attitude. He'd barely kissed his grandmother goodbye at the airport.

"It looks dumb." He turned away from her and faced out the windshield, arms crossed, jaw jutting. "You didn't do it all weekend."

Darian counted to ten before she answered him. That gave her time to think. "You know, I believe you're right. But I suppose I've gotten so used to it I hardly notice it anymore."

The familiar ache between her shoulder blades had slowly gained intensity as she approached Austin and had now reached its customary burn. "I guess I'm just tensing up because I've got a lot on my mind. I told you about my big case, didn't I? I'm a little scared but pretty excited about it." Maybe bringing him a little more into her professional life would help them recapture some closeness they'd enjoyed over the holiday.

"Yeah. So?"

Maybe not.

Monday morning, one week later, when Darian returned from a minor deposition, Marty's enormous eyes and pale face told her something was wrong.

"Darian, thank God you're back. Mr. Huntingdon's called you three times. He cursed at me the last time. Something awful happened in court this morning, and he said he wants to see you the minute you get back." Marty was wringing her hands and she looked miserable and helpless. "And Mrs. Steen called, too. She wants—"

"Call her back, please, and tell her I'll phone her as soon as I'm through with this. Oh, Lord, now what?" Without looking at the rest of her messages, Darian dropped her purse and briefcase at Marty's desk and went straight up to the partners' offices. There was a palpable tension in the air when the elevator doors slid open. She could hear the shouting long before she reached Huntingdon's office, and his secretary waved her in, not even bothering to buzz the intercom.

"...the whole firm," Atwell shouted. "He's lost his mind. He's a senile old son of a...Darian. Where the hell have you been?"

"At Stiles and Overstreet taking the deposition of—"

"Judge Fugate has ordered us to trial in eleven months. Did you hear me? Say something."

Endor Thorogood leaned forward in his chair. "Calm down, Atwell. Take a seat, Darian. As you can see, there's been a change of plans in Goldenair. Everyone is going to have to work faster than we planned. Now this is what we need from you."

An hour and a half later, she walked woodenly out of the office. Richard followed her, looking every bit as dazed as she felt. "We'll be here twenty hours a day. We'll never make it."

"We'll have to make it," Darian said. "The case is too big, but this is going to be a horrible year."

"I can't believe they want that constitutionality memo from you by tomorrow. And how are you going to go through those exhibits in thirty days? There must be thirty or forty boxes of—"

"Fifty," Darian said. "It's not going to be any easier for you. You're on Atwell's team."

"My head hurts," Richard said.

"Mine, too."

"You want lunch?"

"I'll never eat again. I won't have time."

As soon as Darian rounded the corner to her office, her spirits fell even lower. Marty had been crying. Her nose was red and her mascara had made a smudgy raccoon mask around her eyes. "What's wrong now?" She wished her voice would have sounded less exasperated.

"The school called. Twice. The second time it was Dr. Bounds, and he said to tell you if you're not there by two o'clock, they're calling the police."

"*What?*"

"Don't look at me like that. I tried to get through to you, but Roxanne wouldn't take a message in to Mr. Huntingdon's office, and she wouldn't let me go in, either." Marty's voice rose and grew thin and choked. "I don't know. There was a fight or something. Dr. Bounds was really mad and he was talking too fast. I—I couldn't get it down, and when I asked him to repeat, he hung up on me."

"Oh, my God, what time is it?"

"One-thirty."

"I've got to go. Where's my purse?"

"On your chair."

Darian hit her office door with the heel of her hand and flung her legal pad on her desktop. She heard the tentative clickety-click of Marty's heels on the parquet floor behind her. "And Mrs. Steen called—"

Darian whirled around. "For Pete's sake, Marty, I don't have time—"

Her secretary began to shout. "It's your dog. She got out and bit some little girl in your neighborhood. Her parents are going to sue you, and you have to get somewhere with her shot record right away or they're going to put the dog to sleep."

Darian froze. Every thud of her heart pounded through her head with its own skull-splitting intensity. That's all of it, she thought. Everything. Every area of her life had distilled into its own undiluted calamity. For a few seconds, her despair was so exquisitely complete she almost succumbed to the urge to start laughing. My life is now a total catastrophe, she thought. Nothing else can go wrong.

At that moment the phone on Darian's desk jangled. A loud, double ring. She glared at it as if it were a cockroach.

Marty snatched up the receiver. "What?" She listened for a brief moment, and her expression crumpled slightly as she held the phone out to Darian. "It's your mother," she said.

At eight o'clock that night Darian sat in her office staring blankly at an unrepaired nail hole on the wall opposite her. In her right hand, she held a pencil that she was using to methodically drum on the desk blotter.

Some part of her subconscious frantically warned that time was slipping away, but the greater part of her had given over to a numb despair. She had no idea how long she'd been sitting there, staring and drumming, when her office door swung open. She turned her head to look and her soul leaped.

It's you.

He stood still. Just watching her. "Hi." His voice was quiet. The tone was the one most people save for funerals or the hospital rooms of the very sick.

Even when she heard his voice, part of her wasn't sure he was really standing there. "Tom?"

He walked over to her, but didn't touch her. He stopped just short of her chair and propped himself on the edge of her desk. When she looked at him, she knew that he knew, but she had to say it anyway. "Jason was expelled from Fullingham today."

"I know."

"And Mrs. Steen gave her notice. There was some trouble with Winnie—"

"I know. And your case is going to trial sooner than you thought. I know everything. Your mother called me."

"Oh. I don't know what I'm going to do."

He stood and moved behind her chair. "Why don't you just sit there for a minute and let me rub your—good grief. Your shoulders are like rocks."

"I know. They always are."

She hadn't cried. The situation had gone far past tears. But she had to talk. "Winnie didn't bite Shelly Winslow—the little girl. But she's just a puppy and got out and she wanted to play. You know how the boys roughhouse with her. But the more Shelly ran, the more Winnie chased her. And she fell down, and Winnie pounced on her, but she was just playing. Mr. Winslow went completely ape and he screamed at Mrs. Steen. She wanted to quit anyway. Jason's gotten to be too much for her, and she hates dogs.''

It was spilling out like water over a dam. Now that she'd started she couldn't stop. "They expelled Jason. I don't understand. Dr. Bounds wouldn't even let me talk. He said Tykie Wilguneski told him Jason forced him to put paper towels in the drains in the boys' bathroom and then turn on the faucets. But that doesn't make sense. Jason's been terrified of Tykie since he was six. Tykie's huge. He said Jason's been terrorizing him, and taking his money. Can you believe it? I don't believe it. Jason admitted all of it, though. What am I going to do?''

His fingers kneaded the rigid flesh at the base of her neck and down between her shoulder blades. She found herself rocking to the rhythm, and giving in to the pressure. Her muscles surrendered, releasing tension into his broad, warm hands. He never said a word, just murmured soothing noises as if she were an animal he was trying to gentle. He let her talk on until she'd said it all at least twice. Then he moved around in front of her and held one hand out for her to take and led her over to the long, ugly sofa under the windows.

"Please sit here. There's something we need to talk about.''

She finally noticed that he wore a suit—charcoal gray with a brilliant white shirt and a maroon tie. He looked powerful, conservative and unshakably confident. Dressed for a corporate takeover. He didn't look like the Tom she was used to seeing. He could be a senior partner at the firm.

"I've been thinking about this for a while, and I was going to talk to you about it later in the spring, after your partnership review. But, as they say, events seem to have overtaken us." He cleared his throat and looked down, then reached over and took her hand. He didn't twine his fingers between hers although she realized she would have liked that. Instead he just laid her hand palm down against his, then covered it lightly with his other hand. He cleared his throat again.

Maybe not so unshakably confident. What could be bothering him so much?

"I think we should get married."

She didn't answer but tilted her head to one side. I'm not hearing right, she thought. I'm so exhausted I'm having auditory hallucinations. "What?"

One corner of his mouth rose. "I'm asking you to marry me."

She blinked. Twice. "What?"

He smiled and he looked more like himself, happy eyes with the little creases, strong masculine jaw. It seemed as if he'd cleared some hurdle and now he could relax. "I know this seems sudden, but just listen. Although we only met a couple of months ago, we've spent plenty of time together. We know each other. We've become good friends. And we both want to be married, but we both have the same problem. We have no time to get to know someone, to court and all that. I have a funny feeling about this. Like we were meant to meet. You know," he said with a grin. "Destiny."

He paused for a moment and Darian realized her jaw was sagging. She closed it quickly and tried to compose her features. Her eyes were probably bugging completely out of her head. "Tom, I—I—I don't know what to say. I never thought that you—that we...I mean—"

"I know, I know. But just listen to me. There're a lot of good reasons for us to get married—"

"But, Tom, marriage is so...so complicated and hard. The commitment, the bonding that it takes to make it permanent. We've both had marriages that didn't work—"

"Exactly," he said earnestly. "That's why I know this marriage *would* work. We're adults, mature people who care about each other. We have similar demands on our lives, and we're both perfectly capable of living our lives just as they are, but there's something missing."

He gazed directly into her eyes and she could see the unmoving kaleidoscope of his irises. Azure, gray, silver. The pupils expanded to gather the light. They gathered her, as well.

Darian was feeling dizzy. Overwhelmed. "Tom," she began slowly. "What you're saying may be true, but are you sure this would be enough? I mean I know you like me and, I hope, respect me. But are you sure you don't want—"

"My feelings for you go beyond just liking and respect, Darian. I think you're unique. You've got brains and style. And I like your family—Jason and your mother. Don't look at me like that, I really do like Paulina. And besides that, you're gorgeous, and that appeals to my male ego."

That made her smile. There was no doubt they would make a striking couple, and Darian admitted to herself she wasn't beyond a little human vanity. Tom Steinbuck was quite a man. She looked at him, slowly seeing him in a different light. Tall, commanding, respected, and solid and rugged as his land. But what about Tom Steinbuck as a husband?

Her husband. Husband meant wedding. Wedding meant wedding night. She felt the beginnings of a furious blush and dropped her gaze, hoping he hadn't read her expression.

When she looked back up at him, his face had become grave and serious. "I would be a good husband—faithful of course, but I'll also stand by you and support you in your choices. I know what you want from your life, and I admire your commitment to your career and your sense of responsibility to your own abilities. In fact, it's one of the things that attracts me to you the most. You're brilliant and you're determined and successful. You turn your convictions into action. Do you know how few people do that? I'd be proud to be your husband."

It was beginning to sink in. He was serious and this was really happening. Tom Steinbuck was proposing marriage. Her intellect had finally absorbed it. Now other processes had received the information, and she felt an awakening.

Darian lost track of time as Tom spoke earnestly. He'd carefully thought out every possible argument for and against what he was asking, and on all counts marriage seemed the best, most mature and logical solution to both their problems. She had no idea how long he'd been speaking when he paused and took a quick, deep breath.

"...and, like I said, there's Jason to consider. Jason is the kind of son I've always wanted. I think he needs a strong masculine influence in his life." He squeezed her hand. "Not that you're not an excellent mother. It's just that men need male role models. And you wouldn't have to worry about school. There's a really good school in Wimberley. Small, but the academic standards are high, and they've got a great program for gifted kids."

Darian knew she must be tilting her head like Winnie did when she heard a strange noise. "Have you been researching this or something?"

He shrugged slightly. "I believe in being prepared. This school—a lot of its graduates go on to Pipkins when—"

"Good grief, Tom, I could never afford Pipkins."

His smile spoke volumes. *You* couldn't but *we* could.

"And there's more, Darian. Clearpool needs a son. I don't want to think about that place being sold off and divided. It's part of Texas history. It's got its own personality and magic. I want to pass it, and everything that it means, on to my heir, and I want that heir to be Jason."

He looked at the back of his hand resting on top of hers. "I've never told you this, but he reminds me of me. That may sound egotistical, but that's something blood parents come by naturally. They see in their children a reflection and a continuation of themselves and the things they loved and tried to build. In Jason, I see those things, too. He loves the same things I do. And since I'll never have sons of my own blood, I think it really was providence that put him into my life. I think Joel Conroy is an idiot, but if this comes to me because of his stupidity I'll thank God for him."

Darian felt as if an acceleration had commenced inside her, like the escalation of an awakening dynamo. All afternoon she'd suffered from a misery so absolute and yet unfocused she'd felt almost delirious from it. Atwell. Jason. The school. Winnie. For hours her thoughts had been random and fragmented, but Tom's proposal was sinking in, sharpening in her mind with speed and intensity. She could feel the quickening and honing in her emotions along with the throb of her pulse. When she took a sudden breath she realized she'd been barely breathing.

Tom was still speaking. "...And we haven't even talked about our social obligations. Once you make partner, you'll be called on to do more socializing. Lately, I've neglected that in my life, and I know it's going to cost me. We can support each other in so many ways.''

He released her hand. "You want to be part of a family. So do I." His tone reminded her of a lawyer giving a closing argument, summing up and enumerating each point he'd made. "You said you wanted marriage. So do I. This would be a good thing for Jason." He smiled a little and gave her the suggestion of a wink. "And poor little Winnie." He reached into his pocket.

The velveteen box was midnight blue and opened with an elegant little thump.

"Oh, my God, Tom."

It was the biggest marquise diamond she'd ever seen. Surrounded by tiny, perfect sapphires and set on a narrow band, the white stone glittered like a star fallen to earth. When she turned the box, fractured light sprang from the facets like lightning in her hand.

"There is one more thing, Darian. Something important—"

Darian looked at him, and his face was still grave, but somehow more tender.

"—I know we're attracted to each other. I mean, what man wouldn't want you? And I know you feel the same things I feel when we kiss. But I want you to know that I'm a gentle man. I would never hurt you or scare you or want to do anything other than make you happy. There are so many ways I would like to make you happy."

There seemed to be nothing he'd missed. Except maybe...

"Tom," she said softly. "There's one thing we haven't mentioned at all...love."

His eyes seemed to shutter, although he didn't even blink. If anything, he gazed at her more steadily—almost as if he'd been practicing. Like staring into the sun without blinking. "I know what your feelings are about that. We both had marriages based on what we called love. I know you don't want that kind of misery in your life. That hormonal insanity." His gaze did fall then. "Of course, I don't, either. That's why I think this will work perfectly for both of us." He looked up again. "We do care for each other."

"Of course we do," she said. "Even though we haven't known each other for long, I count you among my most trusted friends."

"Well, can you think of any reason why we shouldn't?"

Darian searched Tom's face. What would it be like to wake up seeing him every morning for the rest of her life? Her mouth curved. He offered so much. His strength and resources. A father for Jason. Faithfulness and respect. Security and dignity. A refuge. But more than that—a real home. She realized she, too, had those things to give and more besides. Her companionship and affection— the gentlest female part of herself that had been unappreciated and unwanted for so long.

They would share all these things without the confusion, jealousy and bitterness of romantic insanity. He offered her a partnership based on finer, more lasting emotions and ideals. Darian felt an unravelling inside her, as if for years she had been desperately holding things together by sheer determination, and now she could safely relax her stranglehold on the tenuous threads of her life.

Tears stung the back of her throat and she swallowed. Her eyes were filling, and one salty droplet quivered then spilled from the corner of her eye and slid down her cheek. He reached up with his left hand and touched the warm trail, but he didn't draw his hand away.

He moved closer. "Will you?" he murmured.

His face came toward hers. Her eyes fell to his mouth. He was asking again. The third time. This time with a kiss. *Will you?*

She answered with a kiss.

Yes. Oh, yes.

Chapter Seven

They talked until nearly midnight. At eleven Tom went down to his car and brought back a very good bottle of champagne he'd had chilling in an ice chest.

"You came prepared," Darian said.

The cork made a satisfying pop, and the cool amber liquid gushed into the narrow flutes he'd brought along. As he poured, he gave her a conspiratorial wink. "I was cautiously optimistic."

"I'm glad. This is wonderful."

Darian suddenly found it difficult to look at him, so she studied her left hand. The band was a little large, and she turned the ring with her thumb. She felt Tom gazing at her, and a tingle of anticipation fluttered along her torso. Had they not been at her office, they might have made love earlier. In fact her lips were tender from kissing, and her chin tingled from the roughness of his cheeks. But now, since they were engaged, she felt an odd shyness. Their roles had just changed dramatically, and she wasn't exactly sure what was expected of her. Tom seemed pensive, too.

They sat together on the couch and Darian watched him settle the champagne bottle back in the ice bucket and wrap the damp towel around the neck. Every motion careful and deliberate. Tom cleared his throat. Darian turned the champagne flute in her hand. When he turned to face her, she felt a sudden clutch to her middle, as if she should have been more prepared.

Tom held up his glass. "To a happy, successful marriage."

Darian smiled. "A happy, successful marriage."

They each took a sip. Darian held the cool liquid on her tongue for a moment. Cleared her throat. "I feel like we should be calling people."

"Me, too. But everyone we know is asleep."

"True." She smiled. Then laughed a little. Nervously. "We have a lot of plans to make." She glanced up at him. "When do you think we should . . . How long—"

"Definitely before Christmas," Tom blurted. "I— well, I mean, we'll need to get Jason in school right away and Christmas at the ranch, as a family, I mean . . . don't you think that would be a good start?"

Darian swallowed. Christmas was less than four weeks away. "I do, but that's not much time to plan a wedding."

Tom set his glass down and clasped his hands. "I know. I guess we really do need to work out some details. What about the ceremony? The 'dearly beloveds' and all?"

"The what?"

"You know? The 'Dearly Beloved, we are gathered here' part and all that?"

"Oh," she said, laughing a little. "Let me get this pad. We'll make a list." She picked up a partially used legal pad and flipped to an empty page. "First, the 'dearly beloveds.'"

"You want to do it in a church?"

"I don't know," Darian said and put down her glass. "I don't really see that, do you? I mean some pious, moose-faced clergyman in a cassock and lace surplice intoning the virtues of love undying, obedience and blah, blah, blah with an out-of-tune organ honking out the 'Trumpet Voluntary' in the background. It's not really...us, do you think?"

He shrugged. "I don't know. I'm a believer. I like church. But neither of us go very often, do we?" He rubbed his chin. "We could pay somebody to do it for us? I mean, aren't there people who organize these things for a living?"

"A wedding planner?" Clouds of organdy and pink tulle. Cherubs. The phrase 'Darian and Tom' inscribed in silver italic print on paper napkins. "Ick."

"I know this is not a traditional wedding, but I'd like to have our families there. Maybe a few friends. For Pete's sake, this isn't a leveraged buy-out, it's just a wedding. How hard can it be?"

Darian ignored the exasperation in his voice and gazed over his shoulder and out her window. The moon rode high over Town Lake—not the brilliant Texas full moon, round and white as a dinner plate, but her favorite moon. A bright eyelash carved into the purple sky that left enough velvety darkness for all the stars. And down below that, beyond the jeweled water, street lights lined Congress, and leaped over the Town Lake Bridge before undulating into a vanishing point—out toward Highway 35 and beyond that, the cutoff to Wimberley.

"I want to get married on the porch at Clearpool underneath the mockingbird tree," she said slowly. "You and me and our good friends. And I want to have a barbecue with hot tamales and *cabrito* and a piñata. And music. And I want Dominga to be there, even though she'll cry her eyes out. And Paulina, even though she won't. And I want telegrams from my sisters because I know they can't come. And when everybody leaves I want them to say it was the best wedding they ever went to."

Tom set his glass down and moved toward her, then took both her hands, kissed each palm and looked straight into her eyes. The admiration and affection winnowed toward her in warm waves, and she smiled at him, her eyes returning her gratitude and respect.

"Then, darlin', that's exactly the way it will be. And I know just the lady to plan it. My mother has put on more weddings, wakes and soirees than anyone I know."

"And you're sure your mother won't mind? I mean—" she gestured around her office, at the stacks of boxes and papers and open files "—I won't be much help. I was even planning on paying somebody to do my Christmas shopping."

Tom smiled. "Leave it to Daphne. She loves this sort of thing. Coming to Clearpool makes her sad sometimes because Tuffy's gone, but she's always happy to come home when there's something exciting going on." His smile expanded. "You'll love her. She's Irish. Hell, she gets more Irish as she gets older. Don't let her start telling jokes, though. And whatever you do, don't play cards with her."

Darian laughed. "I never play cards. I wouldn't mind hearing some jokes, though." She was feeling giddy and a little light-headed. "Tom, I feel...strange. Drunk, maybe."

"Me, too. But we've only had a sip." He grinned. "You're just intoxicated with happiness."

Darian pulled her hands away and draped her arms around his neck. "Does the minister or whatever really have to say that 'Dearly Beloved, we are gathered here' stuff? I mean, don't you think it seems silly since this isn't really that kind of thing?"

"Darlin', he can deliver the Gettysburg Address for all I care."

Intoxicated with happiness. Darian felt her smile change. He *had* made her happy. In a way, she felt as if she'd been waiting for this to happen, or as if she'd wanted something without really knowing what it was. Marrying Tom made sense. She would have the best of all worlds. Instead of some childish, fleeting infatuation and hormonal frenzy, she would have a mature commitment, similiar ideals and life outlook—a mutual appreciation of family and tradition. A sensible marriage of like-minded people. No doubt about it, she and Tom were a perfect fit.

"This damn thing doesn't fit. I can't believe it. I'm supposed to walk out there in fifteen minutes and I can't zip this stupid skirt." Darian jerked at the zipper. "Mother, can you?"

"Darian Marie, stop yanking on that. Of course it fits. You've caught the zipper on your slip. Let me—let go. Move your hands. There, what'd I say?"

"Oh. Thanks. Can you help me on with my jacket?" Darian eased her arms into her sleeves, settled the fabric over her shoulders and buttoned the pearl buttons. She turned. "How do I look?"

Paulina Sedgewick was never sentimental. Darian had never even seen her cry, but there was a definite sheen in her eyes when she looked up and down. "Turn, no that way. Yes. Nice. Very nice." She looked straight at Darian. "I must say, Darian, you made an excellent choice."

Darian paused. "You like it?"

"Yes, dear. It's a beautiful suit. Winter white is perfect on you, and simple lines are the most appropriate for an . . . older bride."

"Thanks. I would have felt pretty silly prancing around out here in a wedding gown." Darian looked at her mother. She knew her mother well and had a sneaking feeling that Paulina hadn't been referring to her suit when she said the words "excellent choice."

Paulina sat down in the chair by the bed. "Daphne Steinbuck has done a beautiful job on the flowers. Wait until you see the porch, it's a sea of purple irises and carnations." She sighed. "Although I don't understand why you want that screeching mariachi music. Daphne's been out there encouraging them to play the most unmatrimonial selections."

"She's fun, isn't she?"

Paulina pursed her lips and slanted her eyes away. "Yes. I suppose she's . . . fun."

"I *love* her," Darian said. "You're just upset because she beat you at cards."

"Not fairly," Paulina muttered.

At that moment there was a quiet knock at the door and Dominga peeked in. "Almost time," she said.

Paulina stood and straightened her skirt. She wore a mother's dress of pale pink with a high ruffled collar. Antique lace framed her face and peeked out of her long sleeves.

Darian smiled. "You look like Katharine Hepburn."

"Why, thank you, darling." Paulina flinched a little and turned her head. "What *is* that racket?"

Darian chuckled. "I think that's supposed to be the theme from *Romeo and Juliet.* Sounds different, though, doesn't it? By the way, have you seen Jason?"

"He's been hovering around outside Tom's door. Don't worry, darling, he looks smashing." Paulina checked her watch. "Five minutes."

Darian took a deep breath. "I wish we'd have had a chance to go over the vow part of the ceremony."

Paulina gave her a dry look. "Well, from start to finish, this has been the most untraditional wedding I've ever heard of. No rehearsal. No invitations. No... All right, I know, I've said it all before. Anyway, don't worry. You just have to repeat whatever that doddering old fossil says. You'd better hurry up and get out there. Any second now the poor old thing is likely to keel over dead."

"Oh, be nice. Daphne loves him. He married her and Tuffy forty-something years ago."

"He probably married George and Martha Washington."

"Mother. Be *nice*."

Tom listened to the mariachi music and looked at himself in the mirror. He wore a dark blue suit and black cowboy boots, a plain white shirt and a gray silk tie. His mother had chosen his clothes to go with what Darian was wearing. He was glad Daphne had taken over. The flowers, the food, the announcements—everything. Although both she and Darian had kept him informed about how things had progressed, he had been relieved to be removed from the actual planning of the wedding.

That kind of thing made him feel like a bull in a china shop.

For the past three weeks he'd made appropriate, enthusiastic noises whenever they seemed necessary, but at this moment, he just wanted to get through the ceremony. The tension in his chest made breathing difficult, and he kept having to fight the nagging worry that she'd change her mind.

He'd even dreamed about it. A stupid dream about her handing back the ring because the Hummie was gone and she'd wanted to keep it. Stupid. He hadn't even thought of the Landskimmer since the day he'd met her.

Besides, she'd hated the ATV. Hadn't she? What if she hadn't? That's crazy, he told himself. But there had been other dreams, too. Equally stupid. Equally frightening.

He just knew that he wanted to hear her say the words "I do." Then he could relax. Then the fearful ache in his gut would dissolve and he could get on with the business of making her happy.

There was a soft knock on his door. "Dad?" The door opened.

"Ah," Tom said. "My best man. You're looking sharp."

"Thanks," Jason said and stepped into the room scowling. "Dominga keeps wetting my hair. It looks stupid. I don't wear a part in my hair."

Tom chuckled. "Stay in here. You're safe with me." He paused. "At least I think you are. She may come in here and start wetting us both down. She likes to wash things when she gets nervous. Other than that, how're you making it?"

Jason flopped on the bed. "Okay, I guess. This is pretty fun so far. Everybody keeps asking me where ya'll are going, you know, after." He paused. "I wish you and Mom could have a real honeymoon."

"Well, I do, too, son. We will someday, but your mom is too busy right now."

"I know. She's always busy." He bounced on the bed a little and stuck his legs straight out to study his new shoes. "Dad?"

"Hmm?"

"After you and Mom are married will you have other kids?"

Tom took a moment to study the face so like Darian's, and the sad, serious eyes that tried so hard to conceal vulnerability and fear. He sighed. "C'mere, son." He ruffled Jason's hair back into its normal, shaggy and unparted state. "There, that's better. Now listen to me. No matter what, you'll always be my son. I wish there would be brothers and sisters for you to grow up with, but..." He glanced down, trying to choose his words carefully. "But that probably won't happen, and I hope you're not disappointed someday."

He straightened Jason's tie a little and brushed what looked like cookie crumbs off his lapel. "Do you remember what I said when your mom and I told you we were getting married?"

Jason nodded and his eyes lost some of their wary, guarded look. "You said from that minute on I was your son. That you were my dad—my real dad, and we didn't even have to wait for the wedding or papers or anything. That from then on I was a Steinbuck like you, and I could tell everybody at my new school that Steinbuck was my name."

Jason's gaze fell and his voice grew thin and strained. "And I could call you Dad."

Tom felt his own throat closing, and he reached out and pulled the boy into his arms. "And that won't ever change. I'm the luckiest man in the world. I get to marry your mom and I get to have you for my son. Nothing will ever change that."

Jason pulled away and fumbled in his pocket and brought out a very small package wrapped in tissue. "My grandmother told me that I'm supposed to give you a gift, since I'm your best man and all."

"Well, you didn't have to do that, but thank you."

The boy had obviously wrapped the gift himself, and Tom carefully unfolded the smudged tissue. Folded in the paper, he found a very small oval of sterling silver. One part of it was flattened slightly and he turned it to read the inscription.

Jason swallowed. "It's my baby bracelet. See, there's my name. Jason. When I was a little kid, Mom gave it to me to keep. I—I took it to the mall and had them fix that ring on it so you can put it on your key chain. You know, something to remember me by."

Tom swallowed, carefully folded the tissue closed and put it in his pocket. "Thank you, son. I'll never take it off, I promise. Now come on, let's go get me and your mom married."

The forces of nature had provided a beautiful, crisp but windless December day—almost warm in the sun. The fifty or so guests had spent the past hour mingling, enjoying drinks and sitting at the picnic tables Daphne had ordered.

The ceremony had officially started and Tom now waited, as men throughout time had waited, and tried not to fidget. As he stood in his appointed place on the porch, he watched his mother suspiciously. Daphne's eyes were bright with mischief, and she looked as if she were about to burst into her loud, horsey laughter. She probably was. She stood beneath the oak tree and wore, as she did on all special occasions, emerald green to set off her flame-colored hair. Several middle-aged widowers and bachelors stood close by, shouldering each other resentfully and trying to stand close to her. An adept and incurable flirt, she was obviously in her element.

Tom clasped his hands, forced himself not to look at his watch, and reminded himself not to rock on his heels. Jason was already squirming, and Reverend Cooksey probably couldn't stand up for much longer. Besides being extremely old, Tom recognized a slight glassiness brought on, he suspected, by one or two stiff bourbons. Lena Cooksey, the reverend's unmarried daughter, kept house for him and doled out only the most occasional glass of sherry, so Daphne had no doubt slipped him the bourbon. And also no doubt well out of Miss Lena's undiminished eagle-eye sight.

In only moments, at exactly one o'clock, the mariachis struck up the most eccentric version of the wedding march Tom had ever heard. Paulina walked out—a little stiffly, but that was Paulina. Then Darian appeared and the ache in his chest turned warm. She was really going to do it. She was going to marry him.

He couldn't remember the exact moment when he knew that she was the one. Maybe when they were riding together on Clyde and she'd had her arms around him for so long. No, even before that. He almost felt he'd known her before he'd met her. That he'd been waiting but hadn't realized it. He had never wanted anything so much in his life.

All the unanswered questions in his life were now laid to rest. Here was his future, the resolution of an empti-

ness he hadn't even been aware of until that first day
when she turned around and her hazel eyes pierced him.

She stopped in front of him and he reached out and
took her hand. She smiled up at him.

Reverend Cooksey opened the book he held and
smoothed out the typewritten sheet Tom had given him
earlier in the day. The vows were simple, and there was a
short stanza from a poem by Byron. The old man cleared
his throat and brought his hands very close to his face,
then slowly extended his arms as if playing a trombone.

He tried valiantly to focus. Failed. Then, muttering
something unintelligible to himself, he snapped the book
shut. "Know it all by heart anyway. Done it hunerts o'
times. Don't need some silly paper," he murmured. He
sniffed graciously and looked down his thin, hawklike
nose. "Dearly beloved," he intoned, and raised his arms
benevolently. "We are gathered here..."

Darian began to giggle, and Tom kept a brave, poker
face. He could hear Daphne hooting somewhere off to
his right, but didn't dare glare at her. He'd do that later.
His heart banged hard and slow in his chest, and he was
afraid that when he took Darian's hand he would crush
it.

"I, Thomas Alexander Steinbuck, take you, Darian
Marie..."

When she took his hand to slide the plain gold band on
his finger, he could feel her trembling. Her eyes were
shiny and wide, and when she licked her lips in concentration he felt a punch to his middle. *Can she be nervous? Must be because all these people are standing
around watching. How long do we have to hang around
making nice-nice with these people before we can go?* He
wouldn't rush it, though. He wanted her to remember a
long, happy wedding day. He was also determined to give

her a blissful wedding night. Still, he wanted the ceremony to be over. There was always a chance, even if it was infinitesimal, that she might change her mind.

It wasn't until she looked up at him and said, "With this ring, I thee wed..." that he could finally breathe deeply and easily. Now, he thought, now it begins.

Then it was his turn to place the ring onto her strong, capable hand, and when she said, "I do," there was a flash of joy in her eyes.

Good, he thought. Let her be happy. Please, God, if you're listening, let me make her happy. Let her like it out here. Let her want to come home.

The ceremony was mercifully short, and Tom spent the rest of the afternoon dancing with his wife and visiting with their guests who drank champagne and stuffed themselves on barbecue, Mexican food and wedding cake. At five-thirty the sun had fallen far down in the west, and the evening was turning cold. The remaining guests moved inside the house, and Tom and Darian changed into warm, comfortable clothes.

He was trying to say subtle goodbyes to the lingering and least champagne-soaked of his guests when Reverend Cooksey came tottering over. "Where are you two going on your honeymoon?" the old man bellowed. Tom winced, but knew his years and Daphne's bourbon had finally overwhelmed him.

"Darian can't get away right now because of her job, so we're just going up to the cabin at Clearpool Source," Tom yelled.

"Good man," the reverend whooped, and gave him a broad wink. "In the old days we would have shivareed you all the way there."

Tom bravely returned the old man's wink, while looking around for Lena, hoping she'd bear down on them, full of disapproval and brandishing mugs of strong, black coffee. The last thing he wanted was for his guests to throw together a spontaneous escort out to the Source. He was ready to be alone with his bride.

He'd arranged for the old cabin to be opened, aired and made ready for them to spend the night. Darian said she'd rather stay in the country than in any luxury hotel in Austin. To make the drive to the cabin more romantic, Daphne had borrowed a buggy from one of her friends, decorated it with Christmas garlands and enlisted Rudy to hitch up Clyde as the carriage horse. It was nearly seven when Tom finally caught Darian's eye and gave her the subtle signal to tell her it was time they left.

When they ran outside under a pelting of rice and millet, Tom saw that someone had tied cans and shoes to the luggage straps and hung a very badly painted Just Married sign to the folded canopy. Tom had known his horse long enough to recognize a scathing look.

They laughed and joked with Rudy on the long drive to the cabin. Although Darian didn't kiss him, she did lean her shoulder against him several times and smiled and laughed easily at the outrageous comments Rudy made. The porch light was on, and Dominga's sister, Luz, had built the fire and turned down the bed. She giggled and blushed when she climbed into the buggy beside Rudy, but she turned and called out traditional wedding wishes in Spanish as Clyde clopped away, taking the two of them back to the ranch. Tom had arranged for Rudy to drive out at three the following day to fetch them.

Once inside the cabin, Tom shut the door and turned around. He hadn't been out to the Source in years. The cabin was eighty years old and simple—one large open room with a huge limestone fireplace. The furniture was plain. An old bed made of bird's-eye maple was piled high with homemade quilts. A washstand and chest of drawers. A desk and leather chair under one of the windows. The floor was strewed with old-fashioned hooked rugs, and a long horsehair couch, flanked by chairs, faced the hearth. The kitchen area and a little drop-leaf table were tucked in one corner, and a bathroom had been added in the fifties and updated thirty years later. The place was rustic but snug, and it smelled like winter—pine and wood smoke and furniture polish.

Darian stood by the fire, warming her hands. He hoped she was happy with it. He walked up to stand beside her and could see that she was nervous. His heart was pounding, too. But not from nerves. "Are you okay?"

Her mouth curved, but you couldn't really call it a smile. "I'm fine. Just thinking about the day. It was wonderful, wasn't it?"

"It was the best wedding I've ever been to."

She laughed then. "It was, wasn't it?"

Either the firelight was reflecting brightly on her cheeks or she was flushed. Maybe both, he thought. His own face was probably scarlet. He wanted to suggest . . . but then, again, he didn't want to scare her or push her. "Can I get you anything?"

"Nothing just yet." She looked up at him through thick, dark lashes. "Well, maybe a hug."

Ah, that was what they both needed. She fit perfectly into the curve of his shoulder, and she wrapped her arms around him, holding him to her. Pressing herself close to him. He liked that. Holding her that way and feeling her body smoothed against his. He could feel the thunder of her heart and the swell of her breasts against him every time she breathed. "Do you want to just cuddle here in front of the fire for a while?"

She sighed. "I think that's a good idea. I'll just go freshen up a little."

Twenty minutes later Darian was still in the bathroom. She studied her reflection and saw that her pale cheeks were stained with color. At that moment she wished desperately she'd had less champagne at the wedding. Her head was foggy, but not so foggy that she wasn't knock-kneed from nerves. *Oh, for heaven's sake, go out there and stop hiding in the bathroom. He'll think you're insane.* After all, she knew what to expect. She'd been married before.

At that moment she wished desperately she'd had more champagne at the wedding.

You've faced dozens of juries. You've spoken to whole courtrooms full of people.

Yes, but they all kept their clothes on. I kept all my clothes on, too.

Opening the door took every bit of courage she could muster, but the moment she saw him the knot in her middle relaxed. *This is Tom. The kindest, gentlest man I know. My dear friend. My husband. No matter how inept I am at this, he'll be kind to me.*

He had taken off his jacket and pushed the old couch closer to the fireplace. It looked as if he'd pulled some of the quilts off the bed and made them a nest in front of the fire. Two mugs steamed on the side table alongside what looked like a decanter of brandy.

He smiled at her. "I made some coffee."

"Wonderful. I'm still freezing."

His smile changed. "Well, come over here, then. I've got something to warm you up."

Firelight sent shadows dancing around the room. Darian could hear the low snap and pop of flames devouring the wood. She'd taken off her jacket, and she wore a turquoise cashmere sweater and soft wool pants. Tom wore his usual jeans, but he should have been cold, she thought, since he only had on a dark flannel shirt. No sweater, not even an undershirt. On second thought, she knew why he wasn't cold. The closer she got to him, the warmer the room seemed.

She stopped right in front of him and stood gazing up at his face. The firelight had done something to the blue of his eyes, turned them dark. He didn't move toward her or reach down to hand her the coffee. She didn't move toward the couch. Slowly he reached up and touched her cheek, fingering the spiral curls that hung down at her temple and by her ear. Looking up at him, Darian thought she'd never seen a more perfect masculine mouth. Strong, defined lips. Serious but quick to smile. Tough but generous.

His other hand lifted, grazed her throat and circled around to her nape. He tugged at the pins holding up her hair. She let her eyes drift closed and turned her face just slightly so she could feel his wrist against her skin. She breathed him in and savored and separated each scent— soap, wood, coffee, brandy. She reached out, laid her hands on his sides and sighed. Her hair was falling, aching deliciously as its own heaviness dropped it around her neck and over his mesmerizing hands.

She turned her face a little further and pressed her lips against the inside of his wrist, opened her mouth and tasted him. He moaned and pulled her closer. His hands were already tangled in her hair and now, with tender insistence, they turned her face to his. She didn't open her eyes but remained in the dark, warm place defined by the touch of fire and hands and lips.

She would have lingered in those boundaries for a long time, knowing there would be no interruption, no second thoughts or recriminations. But as soon as the kiss deepened, he moved against her, and the feel of his flat, hard stomach pressing hers ignited something. She flattened her hands on his back, traced the muscles with her hands and explored the deep groove of his spine.

His arms closed around her, pulling her closer. One hand touched her face and almost invaded their kiss, then swept down her neck, over her collarbones and to her breast. She moaned aloud, and his hand closed, feeling and kneading the nub that tightened under his fingers. When he reached beneath her sweater to touch her without the barrier of clothes, she felt a flash of frustration—wanting and needing the feel of his skin against hers.

She reached up to unbutton his shirt, and when she did he smiled down at her, but his eyes conveyed more than pleasure. They held the look of satisfaction, triumph, anticipation.

"Let me," he murmured. When she dropped her arms he didn't reach for the buttons of his own shirt, but for the bottom of her sweater. He peeled it away and dropped it in a shimmering turquoise pool at her feet. Darian started slightly, not frightened, merely surprised. And when he slipped his hands around her to unfasten her bra, she would have helped but again he murmured, "Let me."

In moments she wore only fragile lace panties and firelight, and Tom's kisses were trailing their own fire over her breasts and down her stomach. He knelt in front of her, and were it not for her own escalating pulse and desire, she would have lost herself in studying the chiseled landscape of his shoulders and powerful arms.

His fingers tangled in the filmy lace that circled her hips and slowly peeled the panties down. When he looked

at her he sighed as if he'd been hurt. "You're so beautiful," he said, over and over. She sank to the floor in front
of him, sliding down his body and molding herself
against him. Heat and barely contained passion throbbed
in every feverish embrace as his urgent hands stroked her
stomach, her breasts, her narrow waist and rib cage. With
one more demanding kiss he clasped her to him with one
arm, and with gentle but inexorable strength he parted
her legs to touch the moist darkness between her thighs.

Darian tensed involuntarily. Years had passed since
she'd been touched, and now her blood roared through
her body and she felt herself losing control. Slipping over
a ledge into a kind of voluntary madness she'd never felt
before. Tom never hesitated. His fingers and hands and
tongue never relented in their seduction and enticement.
He only murmured, "Let me."

Hours later, they lay tangled in each other's arms in the
old bird's-eye maple bed. Tom had stoked the fire again,
and shadows danced around them in the room. They had
talked and made love. And talked more, and made love
until the sky grew pale with a winter moon and high, cold
December stars.

"I've never seen my mother cry," Darian said. "Not
even today. I thought she was going to when she was
helping me dress, but then she just got all brusque and
prissy. Like always."

Tom looked thoughtful. "I only saw Tuffy cry three
times in my life. The first was when his daddy died, but
everybody cried at Pappy Steinbuck's funeral. All the
men were blowing their noses and boo-hooing like crazy,
so it didn't scare me. Besides I was just seven or eight.
The last time was when he was in the hospital and he

knew he was dying and didn't want to leave Daphne alone.

"The worst was when I was eleven years old and I wanted to take my daddy's mare swimming. She was probably twenty then, and Tuffy loved that horse in a way I've never seen a man love an animal. Sunshine was famous because she was such a smart mare, part Arabian. Sometimes Tuffy would slip her bridle off and ride her without it. She'd obey his voice commands."

Tom sighed, and pushed his hair away. When his hand left the warm, damp skin of Darian's stomach, she felt almost bereft. She wanted to take his hand and press it back against her body, but she felt oddly shy. He stared toward the fireplace for a moment and she said nothing, just waited and watched as the firelight played across his face.

"She didn't want to go in, but I made her and she had a heart attack. She died in the water. We had to get a truck to pull her up onto the bank."

"Oh, Tom, how awful."

He tilted his head in the suggestion of a shrug. "Tuffy was heartbroken. I was scared out of my mind that he'd hate me forever. He just held her head in his lap and cried. We never even talked about it, and I knew there was nothing I could do to make up for what I'd done. I just had to learn to live with it."

Darian reached up and touched his jaw, backlit by the fire and beginning to roughen with sandy stubble. "That's why you wanted to have Jason work at the ranch, isn't it? So he wouldn't feel so bad about wrecking that ATV?"

"I suppose that's part of it. I know what it's like to be unable to make up for something you've done." He looked down at her face. Then her nipples, still glowing and swollen from their lovemaking. Slowly a smile transformed the grave planes of his face from sadness to something else. "Of course I did have other reasons."

His fingers trailed over the angle of her hipbone and followed the curve of that hollow down toward her tangle of damp curls. His hand slid under her thigh and teased up her knee as he moved on top of her. "I'm glad you don't need much sleep."

She smiled lazily and let her hands glide up the ridges of his rib cage, through the springy hair of his chest to the crest of his powerful shoulders. "Me, too."

By the end of December the hill-country landscape turned dry and bleak—gray rocks scattered on tufted yellow grass. Black, leafless trees splayed against a high thin sky. Darian loved it. Every time she made the drive, she appreciated even more the stark landscape and the quiet time she spent after she left the firm and headed for her home.

She could chart the progress of the drive by the time it took to reach each landmark or by the slow, predictable unraveling of the tension in her body. When she left the Austin city limits, the ache in her neck eased. At Munchak's Feed and Grain, her shoulders began to relax, and by the time she pulled up next to Tom's truck, she almost felt as if she'd had a hot bath.

When she killed the engine and stepped down, Winnie barreled around the side of the house and sent Dominga's fat white chickens flapping and squawking across the dry yard. The pointer wiggled and pawed and made general havoc of Darian's panty hose, while trying to simultaneously present both her head and backside to be scratched.

"Down, Winnie," Darian scolded. "Winnie, down. Damn it. Look what you're doing to my...oh, hell."

She dropped her purse and briefcase on the antique hat stand in the entry and walked through to the family room.

Tom lay on the most comfortable couch, reading an oil-and-gas journal. A watery Scotch sat at his elbow, and he'd built a fire in the fireplace. The logs snapped and settled in the grate as the mellow light of the fire painted the room in warm colors.

The way he looked when he saw her spoke volumes. She smiled at him through a blush of pleasure.

He stood and crossed to her. "You're home early."

"Yeah, I thought I'd surprise you. I'm really caught up today, and the stuff I have to do can be done here."

He kissed her on the mouth. Again. "My life gets better all the time," he said. "I have to be the luckiest man in the world. A gorgeous, sexy, brilliant woman actually comes to my house and sleeps with me. Several times a week even."

She laughed a little. "She wishes she could come to your house every day, and looks forward to the day when she never sees another airline invoice or travel-agent complaint. She's so sick of reading thousands of ticket stubs she could pull all her hair out."

He smiled. "Let me," he murmured. "God, I love doing this."

"Now what do we have today?" He said in mock concentration as he reached up and gently tilted her head forward. "This is nice." He uncoiled the braid she had pinned in place on the top of her head, then undid it and combed his fingers through the heaviness, massaging her scalp with his thumbs. "How's that?"

"Feels wonderful," she murmured, and ran her hands lightly up and down his strong flanks. She sighed, let her eyes drift down and hooked her thumbs into the top of his pants.

His hands made strong, familiar magic with circular strokes that turned her neck and shoulders to liquid butter. "Where's Jason?"

"Stargazing with Rudy and Eddie. There's some celestial something or other supposed to take place around eight-thirty."

"So we're alone for the next two hours?"

He ran his hand under her chin, tilted her head back and dropped another light kiss on her upturned mouth. "Completely," he murmured.

"What would I have to do to get you to fix me a drink and meet me in the hot tub?"

"I'll think of something," he said.

Long after midnight Darian woke up, slipped out of bed and into her robe. Tom slept in a pool of moonlight, one muscular arm thrown back and the other resting on his stomach. As usual, he'd kicked the covers free from the bottom of the bed so he wouldn't feel bound in by them. Emotion swelled in Darian's chest. She turned away and left the room as quietly as she could.

Everything has settled into place, she thought. All the tangled threads of her life, the loose ends, had been picked up and woven together into a fabric of contentment. She trusted Tom's commitment to their marriage and believed in his integrity. Even when they disagreed, he fought fairly—vigorously but without any hint of meanness. Just as they had agreed, their marriage was one of quiet satisfaction, mutual admiration and continuing physical delight.

She smiled to herself as she walked through the house, glanced out the windows to the clear, cold night and checked the doors. She peeked in Jason's room and saw him sprawled on his bed with the total lack of inhibition that only the young retain. Winnie raised her head, but didn't jump off the bed to greet her.

I don't know what I did to deserve this, but thank you. My life is perfect. I want to live this way forever. Please don't let anything change. Ever.

This marriage was nothing like her first. Tom was certainly nothing like Joel Conroy. Maybe that part of her life had been an ugly test or gauntlet she'd had to run to earn this life. She thought of Joel's casual infidelities, his indifference and mockery of her values and her abilities. Even in bed. Was she so different now? she wondered. No, no one changes that much.

Tom was simply a superior man. Faithful and honorable. He respected himself and therefore treated those around him with respect. He was honest and not afraid to say exactly what he thought. Or what he wanted. Even in bed. She smiled then.

She'd never felt sexier, smarter or more desirable than she did since she married him. Not as a teenager and not in her twenties. Here she was, a grown woman well past girlhood, but she couldn't walk into a room without him devouring her with his eyes. And if Jason was away, his hands and mouth.

Maybe they weren't in love, but he treated her with a hungry but tender passion she knew most lovers never experienced. Afterward, he always held her. Stroked her. And said the most outrageous things. She blushed just thinking of it.

When she slipped back into bed, Tom murmured a greeting and wrapped her in his arms. Heaving a sleepy sigh, he asked, "Where've you been?"

"I'm sorry I woke you. I thought I heard something."

"I didn't hear anything, and I'm a light sleeper."

"I know." She snuggled against him and lightly traced the angle of biceps into the fold of his elbow. She smiled, knowing how this kind of touch made him feel. His hand flattened against her stomach, pressing her against him and the rhythm of his breath changed.

He pushed himself up on one elbow and brushed her hair away from her face. "Was everything all right? I mean, what did you hear?"

"It was nothing," she said softly. "It had to be my imagination." She laid her hand on his face, guiding his mouth down to hers.

She would have said more, but his mouth covered hers and soon her thoughts were driven from the imaginary noise that had disturbed her sleep. For a fleeting instant she thought she'd remember and ask in the morning if anyone else had heard it—an odd sound so far out in the country.

Just one warning clang.

Chapter Eight

"Hi, Marty. Welcome back."

"Hello, Darian. Wow, you look terrific. Married life must agree with you."

Darian didn't bother to try to hide the blush she felt rising. Even after nearly two months, reference to her marriage still caused a rush of emotion to color her cheeks. "Thanks for saying so. It's been . . . good."

Marty raised her eyebrows dramatically. "Good? You're absolutely blooming. Even with all the Golden-air nuttiness. I thought when I came back you'd be bent and haggard."

Darian laughed. "Well, I'm folded, spindled and mutilated on the inside, I'm just putting on a brave front." She sighed. "It *has* been chaos, though. You've been missed. I've been through three floating secretaries and two temps since you've been gone. They've got some horrible nickname for me, and no one will tell me what it is."

"Ooh, I'll find out and blackmail you." Marty smiled, set her purse down and looked ruefully at the stacks of mail and files on her desk. She sighed. "It's nice to know I was missed. I guess."

"How was Colorado?"

Marty sighed. "Bliss. Four weeks is not enough, though. When I win the lottery I'm going to spend the rest of my life chasing ski bums." She sent Darian a wistful smile. "I'd love a cup of coffee and some catching up before I tackle this. Do we have time?"

"No, but let's take time. Put your stuff down and meet me in my office."

When Darian shoved open her office door Marty was standing in the middle of the room, gazing unhappily at the stacks of boxes. "This is horrible," she said. "What is all this junk?"

"Exhibits," Darian said. "You should see Richard's office. It's a maze."

Marty took the cup from Darian. "Thanks. Now tell me, how was Christmas? And New Year's?"

Darian told Marty everything that had transpired since the wedding. The Christmas parties. New Year's Eve at the Driskill. Jason's new school and his tutor. How Rudy had inexplicably developed a crush on Paulina and, no matter how scathing her comments, trailed around after her whenever she came to the ranch. Singing her cowboy love songs or leaving her very bad poetry.

Winnie had come into season and had to be locked in the utility room for a week. Every night her mournful howls echoed all through the house, while every loose male dog in a ten-mile radius of Clearpool skulked around outside, love-crazed and vigilant.

One night during the first week in January, about twenty of the cows had broken through the fence, and the men rounded them up by moonlight on horseback, using the Hummies Tom had bought for Christmas despite Darian's furious protests. Jason was allowed to help, and Darian had never seen him prouder of himself than at three o'clock that morning as he came in from the freezing night with the other men. They stomped in, their cold muddy feet ruining Dominga's kitchen floor, noisy, whacking one another on the back and generally congratulating themselves about how wonderful they were.

Darian had felt as if she'd stumbled into some male tribal ritual, and had taken herself back to bed. Although she'd faked a tough stance and scolded them all about leaving the mess for Dominga, she secretly carried with her the image of Jason's joyful, windburned face. He seemed taller, tougher and more confident—less surly and boyish. He laughed more now, and they hardly argued at all anymore.

"You're lucky," Marty said. "There's a lot of men who don't get along with their step-kids."

"I know," Darian murmured. "But it's not even like Tom is Jason's stepfather. He's more like his real father than, well, lots of real fathers I've seen."

Marty shook her head and stood up. "You're the luckiest woman I know." She picked up Darian's empty cup. "Not that you haven't worked hard and earned everything you have, but you've got the perfect life. Great career. Gorgeous, wealthy husband who's great to your son." She laughed. "And, of course, the best secretary in the world."

Darian paused for a moment. Some vague protest had almost materialized inside her, but she couldn't quite get it into focus. She rolled her eyes. "Well, then get out there and get to work before I have you chained to your oar."

"Right."

* * *

Darian spent the rest of January and the first two weeks in February organizing expert witness testimony, interviewing witnesses and working on discovery answers. Almost every day she ate lunch at her desk, the routine varying only on days when she had to be in court. All the associates and partners working on Goldenair ate at their desks—usually both lunch and dinner, and even though the receptionists tried to provide variety, the delivery-service food lost its appeal within weeks. Pizza. Chinese. Italian. Mexican. No matter how good the food might have tasted in the restaurant, eating it from cardboard carryout containers diminished its appeal. Darian had also begun to feel some telltale tightness in the waistband of some of her fitted skirts and dresses. Sitting at her desk for fourteen hours a day was obviously taking more than a mental toll.

At five-thirty one Wednesday afternoon her phone rang and she smiled when she reached for it. Tom always called at the same time. "Darian Steinbuck."

"What a nice name, Mrs. Steinbuck. I'll bet you're married to a wonderful man."

"You'd win that bet." She leaned back in her chair and wound the cord through her fingers. "How are you?"

"Beat to a bloody pulp. I've been in Austin since eleven, trying to get this damn merger hammered out, and I'm about to yank out my hair. You lawyers. I'm telling you, if I wasn't married to one—"

"Are you maligning my honorable profession? Let's talk about robber cattle barons, land-grabbing frontier industrialists and—and—"

"Okay, okay. Would you care to trade insults over dinner?"

"Dinner? Do you mean real dinner? On real plates? With salt and pepper you don't have to tear open?"

"I do. And yes, I know—I spoil you rotten."

"True. But I like that in a man."

"Is seven good?"

"Eight is better."

When he walked through the door and she saw him, she was hit by the same reaction as always. The hitch in her breath, the smile she couldn't suppress, the flutter that felt like laughter trying to escape. Part of the joy she felt was seeing herself reflected in his handsome face—the delight and masculine admiration. The sexy glimmer that never failed to ignite in his eyes when his gaze traveled down her body.

Their greeting had become a ritual. No words, but as always, he paused at the door for a moment, smiled, then without speaking walked over to her chair, bent down and kissed her full on the mouth. His left hand teased through her hair and with practiced efficiency, dragged the clip loose and massaged her hair free. His right hand cupped her chin, but soon made its lazy trail down her throat to find her breast to squeeze gently. And then with more urgency.

"Hello, counselor," he murmured against her lips.

"You taste good," she replied as her fingers traveled down his cheek to stop close to his lips.

"You must be very hungry to like the taste of stale rancher."

"Starving." She laughed. "But you do taste good."

"Well, then," he said, straightening up and leaning against her desk. "Instead of eating out, how would you like room service?"

"Did you get our favorite—"

"I sure did. It's the full moon, and I know how you like that view."

A warm, familiar sensation curled through Darian's torso. Ever since they'd been married, Tom tried to stop by at least twice a week to take her to dinner. And at least once a week, without fail, he would take the bridal suite at the Fallbrook, the magnificent luxury hotel facing Town Lake. There would be champagne chilling, and scented oil foaming in the hot tub. And satin sheets on the king-size bed. Afterward, Tom returned to Clearpool and often waited up for Darian to come home.

"There's something so wicked about taking a hotel room for a few hours," Darian said, and laughed a little. "Do you think the staff thinks I'm your mistress?"

Tom grinned. "I hope so. I love the looks on the faces of all the men. They hate me. I can just see them asking 'What's that old warthog doing with that gorgeous lady?'"

She looked at him. Chiseled ruddy features. Happy lines flanking clear blue eyes. Dark ruffled hair. Broad shoulders and strong hands. "You know what, Tom? Suddenly I'm not very hungry."

The smile left his mouth, but not his eyes. "Come on then," he said quietly. "Don't make me wait any longer."

At ten-thirty, they sat together in Tom's car outside Darian's office. He stroked a stray wisp of hair back over her ear and smiled a little. "I wish you didn't have to go back."

"Me, too. I have about two more hours of work and then I'll head home."

"You're not too tired to drive, are you? Because if you are, I'd just as soon you—"

"No," she laughed shyly. "You know how . . . this energizes me."

He grinned slyly. "This? What do you mean *this*?" He took her hand and guided it down. "Do you mean this?"

She snatched her hand away and wrapped it behind his neck. "Stop that, you fiend. Kiss me and let me go, or I'll never get home."

"All right." He sighed and ran his hand affectionately down her neck and over her shoulder. "I'll see you at the house."

She hesitated. "Does this . . . bother you? Me being gone so much I mean?"

His eyes cut away from hers immediately, and he appeared to be carefully choosing his words. "I'm happier than any man has a right to be. We discussed this a long time ago. We both know what this trial means—it'll guarantee your partnership." He glanced at her briefly as if checking for something. "Jason is okay with it right now. In spite of all the changes, he's adjusting. All of us know that for the next few years your career is going to be really demanding. I—we accept that." He took a quick breath and gave her another quick glance. "And, of course, you're not the only one who's busy." His words were blurted, as if he were making an excuse. "I mean, we both know what it's like for me, too—"

"Of course," she said. "Your life is every bit as demanding as mine. I just didn't want . . ."

He looked at her. "What?"

She dropped her gaze. Somehow the fact that he was so content made her feel wistful. Or dissatisfied. *Don't be stupid. Like Marty says, you have the perfect life.* "Oh, nothing." She kissed him lightly. "I'm procrastinating. I'll see you at home around midnight." When she stepped out of the car, she turned around and winked. "Save me the warm spot."

He winked back. "Always."

When her desk clock chimed midnight, she took off her glasses, rubbed her eyes and decided to go home. Tom's voice was thick with sleep when she called home to tell him she was leaving. She hated waking him up, but he insisted that she never drive home without phoning him first.

When she walked in the kitchen door, Winnie bounded down the hallway, wiggling and exuberant. As Darian bent over to pat her, the dim kitchen light showed that Dominga had left her a note. In the refrigerator she would find a plate of chicken ranchero with jalapeño corn bread and a little crockery bowl of black bean soup. Darian was starving and queasy from too much coffee, and her stomach ached at the mere sight of the home-cooked food. She put the chicken and rice in the microwave, set the timer and walked quietly into the living room.

Tom was asleep on the longest, widest couch with Jason curled up against him. He'd obviously built a huge fire earlier in the evening, and the embers painted the two of them where they lay tangled together in matching gray flannel warm-ups. A book splayed open on Tom's chest; Jason's hair was a ratty unkempt mess. Apparently Tom, as usual, hadn't made him blow it dry after his shower. Even in sleep Tom's arm curved protectively around her son, holding him close in case he might roll away and fall. Darian felt herself wanting to cry—as if something wonderful had taken place, and she had missed it. Hadn't even been invited.

She sighed aloud, and Tom's eyes fluttered, squinted. He checked his watch. "Hi," he whispered.

"Hello," she mouthed. "What is Jason doing in here?"

"He came in when he heard the phone. He wanted to wait up for you." He lifted his other hand and motioned for her to come to him. To kiss him. "Your eyes are red."

Darian smiled quickly and made a dismissive little flap with her hand. She swallowed. "Eye strain."

He gazed at her for a moment, studying her, it seemed, then he looked away. "Well, shall we put this boy in a bed?"

"Yes. Oh, I've got some food heating in the micro-wave and—"

"Oh. Okay, after you eat I'll meet you in the bed-room. Nice room. First door on your left," he joked.

"See you there," she said. But by the time she'd eaten, put away her dishes and showered, Tom was asleep. His face was smooth and relaxed, and his left hand rested palm-down across his bare chest.

His wedding band glimmered against his brown skin with its own dull light. As Darian slipped quietly into bed beside him, she wondered how long he'd lain awake before he got tired of waiting for her.

On Sunday Darian turned onto the Dripping Springs cutoff and snapped off her hand-held recorder. She'd thought she remembered the cite she needed, but it had slipped her memory. She dropped the little tape recorder on her seat beside her and rubbed the back of her neck. The feeling was so familiar. Every time she was headed to work it was the same—the escalating tingle that turned into a dull ache, then a burn. But this time was differ-ent. She swallowed and bit her lip. Rolled her shoulders and rubbed at the aching muscles. Her breath hitched a little, and she said a word she used only in her most frustrated moments.

She wasn't headed toward Austin and the office. She'd been at the office all day and now she was going home.

She was headed toward the ranch, and instead of becoming more relaxed in anticipation, she felt the tension in her shoulders intensifying to a fiery ache. Finally, when the pain and frustration were too much to ignore, she pulled over at the first scenic cutaway in the road, leaned her head against the steering wheel and let herself cry.

"What's wrong with me?" she said aloud. "What's wrong?" She stepped out of the four-wheel drive, slammed the door hard and walked around to lean against the quarter panel. "I have the perfect life," she shouted at the valley, and raised her clenched fists. "I'm going to make partner. Jason has never been happier, and I'm married to a wonderful man. I have a great career, financial security—everything I said I wanted. I have the perfect life." As soon as the words left her mouth, she wanted to collapse.

Different words had been growing inside her for weeks, swirling and condensing like a gathering hurricane while she functioned desperately in its invisible eye. She knew if she said the words aloud they would take on a dangerous purpose of their own and cut a path of destruction across the landscape of her oh-so-perfect life.

But trying to hold them in was useless and she knew it. She gave up, and dropped her face into her hands. "I hate my life. I hate my life." Over and over again through her tears, she said the traitorous words and let the high hillcountry wind blow them away. "I made a mistake. I hate my life."

She cried until she'd cried it out, and the exhaustion of spent tears calmed her. *But what is it exactly that I hate?*

What is wrong? The answer was simple. She'd known it for weeks, but she wouldn't admit it. "I love him. I'm in love with my husband."

The irony of the situation struck her, and she laughed bitterly. "I am in love with my husband, and that will probably ruin my marriage."

How did I miss this? How could I have been so stupid? But she knew she hadn't missed it. All along—even from the first moment—there had been something powerful between her and Tom. But she'd been determined not to see it. She'd volunteered for blindness because loving him interfered with what she thought was her duty. Her responsibility.

Her strength and independence.

Or was there more to it than that? Had the role of the efficient professional just been a disguise all along? Was the truth that she was really, at her most basic center, a spineless, dependent weakling? And if anyone discovered the truth about her, she would be abandoned again. Just as her father had done. And Joel. Was that it?

The truth of it resonated through her. She hadn't wanted to love someone—to be dependent. To love is to lose. That was the weakness she'd managed to hide for years under a veneer of competence and control.

And it was all true. She *did* want to quit.

"Oh, God," she muttered. "I'm as bad as what's-her-name. His ex-wife. I want to be a clingy, stay-at-home hausfrau. I'm probably worse than she ever thought about being. I'm as bad as Joel. Deep down I bet I just want to quit and have Tom take care of me. Of us."

She swiped her hand across her eyes. "Ugh." Mascara trailed a runny black streak from wrist to knuckle. "No telling what I look like," she muttered. "This is stupid." She pulled the clip out of her hair and let the wind whip it around her face. "I don't have to give in to this. Anyway, it's too late to change things even if I could. Besides, *he* is happy with the way things are." She felt a surge of anger. Of course he is, she thought. He's got everything. A fortune. The ranch. *My* son. A smart, successful wife who adores him. He probably knows it, too; he just acts like he doesn't. He's bound to know how I feel; he just doesn't want the deal to change.

"Oh, be fair," she said aloud. "This is what you said you wanted. You better snap out of this and be grateful for everything you've got. So you're in love with him. He's a wonderful man, the best father you've ever seen. And, besides, you get to be around him. Sometimes. You'd better straighten up or you'll lose everything you do have."

On the way home she stopped at a service station and washed her face in the bathroom. Her eyes looked swollen, she thought. In fact her whole face looked puffy. Who'd ever be in love with you? she asked herself blackly. You'd better be grateful for what you have. If you start complaining now, you'll ruin what happiness you've got. Now put on a courtroom face. You don't have the right to make everyone else miserable just because your husband doesn't... But she couldn't finish the thought without making herself cry again. She started the car, turned on the radio and sang as loud as she could until she pulled in at the ranch.

Tom and Jason were sitting at the kitchen table when she walked in. She stretched her mouth into a smile. "Hello, men," she said. Her voice sounded brassy and fake.

"Mom!" Jason jumped up and threw his arms around her. "You're home early."

Tom stood, put his arm around her shoulders and kissed her lightly. "Hello, counselor. This is a nice surprise." He looked straight into her eyes. "Are you all right?"

For one instant she felt the tears clawing at her throat, but she whipped her gaze away. "Fine," she said. "Beat, though." She ruffled Jason's hair. "How was your day?"

"Great, we found two arrowheads. I'm doing a report for school. Lemme show you." He turned and tore off toward his room.

"Don't run in the house," she called. She might just as well have said it to Winnie.

"Dominga made dinner," Tom said quietly as he pulled a casserole out of the refrigerator.

"That was sweet. Even on her day off."

"Wasn't it? Look, fettucini Alfredo."

"I can't eat that," Darian snapped. She surprised herself with the ugliness in her voice, and was just going to apologize when Tom faced her, his eyes hard, expression cold.

"What's wrong with it? I thought you liked Italian. She did, too. That's why she made it." He set the dish down so hard the lid clattered.

Darian looked at the floor. *I'm not going to cry.* "Oh. I—I'm worried—I've been eating so much rich food. I'm sure I've gained ten pounds." She looked up at him. "Do you think I'm getting fat?"

His eyes widened in surprise, but remained suspicious. Offended. "What?"

"Do you? Do you think I'm gaining weight?"

His gaze dipped away. "Those are two different questions."

I knew it. "Well?"

He cleared his throat. "Yes, I think you've gained weight, and, no, I don't think you're fat. You were too thin."

"Why didn't you ever tell me you thought I was bony?" *Please shut up.*

He took a deep breath and curled both hands into fists. "I'm going out to the barn, Darian." His voice remained calm. "If you want me, I'll be back in about an hour." He didn't wait for her to answer, but turned and left. He didn't even stop to get a jacket.

Jason bounded back into the kitchen, eyes alight and face glowing with excitement. He held out two perfect flint arrowheads. "Dad took me riding this morning and we found them in the creek bed." He looked around the kitchen. "Where'd he go?"

I hate myself.

Later that night when she slipped into bed beside him, she knew he was awake. He never slept turned away from her.

"Tom?"

"Mmm?"

"I'm sorry."

He sighed heavily, rolled over and gathered her to himself, turned her gently until his knees nested behind hers and his breath curled warmly into her nape. "It's okay. I know you're tired."

She lay there beside him just as she had lain night after night for nearly three months. Before she'd always felt safe and warm. If not loved, at least cherished and appreciated. Now his arm felt too heavy; his muscular leg a burden across her thigh. The food she'd eaten had sunk like lead in her stomach and everything—Tom's body, the covers, the light gown she wore, all seemed suffocating and oppressive.

She waited until his breath grew even, his body relaxed and heavy. Then she eased herself away, curled herself around her pillow and softly cried herself to sleep.

The next morning, she didn't feel any better. Worse in fact. She woke up unrested and nauseated. She felt light-headed and disoriented, but she had no temperature.

Tom's face grew dark with consternation even when she showed him that the thermometer registered normal. "When was the last time you went to the doctor?"

Her gaze slid away and she chewed the inside of her mouth. "Uh, September."

His eyes narrowed. "What year?"

Damn. "Look, Tom, I'm sure I'm just tired—"

"I'm sure you are, too. You work fifteen hours a day." His voice rose. "You know that exhaustion is the single most determining factor in breaking down your immune system."

"I'll be fine."

"Are you going to stay home and rest today?"

"I can't do that."

"Well, then, you're going to the doctor. You need a checkup anyway for the insurance."

She took a deep breath but could see there was no point in arguing with him. "Okay, I'll make an appointment." *That doesn't mean I'll keep it.*

He crossed his arms. "Good. I'll drive you."

At eleven-thirty they sat in the waiting room of Tom's general practitioner. Dr. Maggie Winstrom had been Tom's family physician for years, and she'd shuffled her other appointments so Darian could come in. Still, the tests all took longer than Darian had hoped. The prodding, poking and general indignities of the examination had done nothing to improve her state of mind, and she squirmed impatiently on the leather divan. Picking up a two-month-old magazine, she heaved a sigh and rolled her eyes dramatically at Tom, who ignored her.

The nurse opened the door and looked into the waiting room, her face grave. "Mrs. Steinbuck, can you come back and see the doctor for a moment?"

Darian stood quickly and dropped her purse. Why did she look that way? she wondered. Oh, God, what's wrong with me? Nobody in my family lives long. Well, that's not true, but...

The waiting-room door thudded ominously behind her, and the nurse motioned into Dr. Winstrom's private office. The first thing she noticed was the box of tissues sitting dead center on the doctor's desk.

"Darian," she said, smiling sympathetically. "Please sit down."

Fifteen minutes later when Darian walked back into the waiting room, she knew her face was pale. Tom looked up, saw her expression and his face lost all its color. "What is it?"

"Do you know a good lunar meteorologist?"

"What? What do you mean?"

She tried to smile, but the corner of her mouth jumped. "Remember when you said the likelihood of you fathering a child was roughly equal to the chances of it raining on the moon?"

She made it all the way to the couch, but then her knees gave out and she sat down heavily. "Well check the lunar forecast, darling. We're going to have a baby."

Chapter Nine

That night they deliberately left the curtains open, and Darian lay in the crook of Tom's arm, staring up at the ceiling. The moonlight pouring through the trees cast shadows of filigree and spiderwebs, and bathed their naked bodies in benign silver light.

Tom had been unable to take his eyes off her, and every time he laid his broad hand on her stomach, the corners of his mouth rose, and his delight moved through him visibly.

"My whole family has always been fertile," Darian said. Again. "I told you I got pregnant with Jason on my honeymoon." She realized she was still slightly in shock. They both were. They'd taken the rest of the day off and spent it together in bed. "I told you about my mother. How easily she got pregnant. And Johanna. I can't believe it. It must have happened on our honeymoon. I never worried about being late, you know, my period and all. I was so busy. I told you—"

"Hush," he said and put his finger on her lips. "You're working yourself up into a state. You're going to start crying again."

She cut her eyes toward him. "What's wrong with that?" *Don't snap that way.*

He just smiled down at her. "Doesn't bother me at all. But you keep saying how ugly you feel when your face is puffed up. I think you're beautiful." He trailed his hand upward between her breasts, tracing the curve of her collarbone, circling her breast until gooseflesh rose and made her nipples pucker. Then down again to rest on the hint of a swell beneath her navel. Again, he smiled and stared, resting his hand, flat and warm, against her belly.

"I wonder what they'll say at the office. I wonder if this'll make any difference to the partners." *Tell me to quit. Tell me to hand in my resignation.* "Sometimes it does."

Tom's smile faded. "You don't have to say anything yet. If you don't want to. They're supposed to announce partnerships the first of April, right? That's only about a month away."

"Right," she said quietly.

"Of course, I think you ought to slow down some."

"Do you?"

"I sure do. I'm phoning the Fallbrook tomorrow and taking a six-month lease on the suite. I want you to be able to rest anytime you need to."

Darian swallowed against the tightness in her throat. *How considerate.*

"And if it gets too late, you won't have to drive home at all. You can keep plenty of clothes there." He smiled. "You'll need lots of new clothes, won't you?"

"Probably," she whispered.

His fingers eased back up over her ribs, to one rosy areola. He raised his fingers to his mouth, wet them and touched her again. She moaned and arched against him.

Soon, with him inside her, filling her with his sweet, powerful magic, she was unable to bite back tears. If he felt a difference in the way she sobbed against his chest, he didn't say, but afterward, even more than usual, he held her and stroked her tenderly.

She, of course, said nothing. After all, what did she have to complain about? Now she had even more than she ever said she wanted.

For the next two weeks, Darian tried to pace herself at work and to take time during the day to get up and walk. She ate the huge, nasty-tasting vitamins her new obstetrician prescribed, and drank lots of water. She sneaked copies of magazines about motherhood and maternity into her office and read them behind locked doors. She didn't dare even tell her sisters she was pregnant because she knew they'd tell Paulina, who would probably swoop down and terrorize them all for months.

Tom came to town even more than before, and Darian thought he was looking tired. She knew there had been some shake-ups in banking and the oil field, and she was vaguely aware that Clearpool's holdings were multinational and complicated. After all, the prenuptial agreement they'd signed was as thick as a metropolitan phone book, but she attributed his tiredness to the fact that he was probably as dazed by the pregnancy as she was. For a few days, they'd been like children sharing a secret, but then some other energy had taken over. He'd grown pensive and a little distant.

Darian sat at her desk, staring at the unrepaired nail hole and drumming with her pencil. She rested one hand on her stomach. She wore her least favorite blazer over her largest skirt, which she held together with a long safety pin. Her breasts were tender, and certain smells sent her running for the bathroom. Bacon. Frying onions. Cooked cabbage.

She imagined her baby, tumbling and flexing in the warm pocket underneath her heart. Fluttering inside her womb like a butterfly. *It's a little girl. I know it is.* Darian pressed her lips together, willing back her tears. Already she loved the life inside her. The baby that was part her and part Tom, and more than the sum of both of them. She wanted a different life for this baby, a different set of rules and demands. Everything in her wanted to protect the little life from anything that would cause pain. *Then talk to your husband. Give him a chance.*

Darian sat up straight. "Good grief. How simple." She smiled. Then laughed. "Of course, I've never even talked to him about this. Maybe if he knew I'd changed my mind about things, he'd understand. Who knows? Maybe he feels different, too."

She decided to go home early, and checked her watch. It was barely six o'clock. She could finish this memo, pack up a couple of files and be home in time to sit down and have dinner with Tom and Jason. Her son had surprised everyone with his enthusiasm over the baby. He and Tom even seemed to share a pact or secret agreement about Jason's new brother or sister. She reached for the phone to call them, then changed her mind. It would be a surprise. She could imagine the looks on their faces when she showed up with big, fat steaks to barbecue. A little red meat just this once wouldn't hurt. And a soup bone for Winnie, too.

She worked quickly, trying to muster more concentration than normal. The memo was in fair shape, just a couple more passes should do. She took her purse out of

the file drawer and set it on the floor by her trial briefcase. The top of the briefcase yawned open, like the
mouth of an unfed animal, and Darian squared the corners of her papers carefully before stuffing them inside
along with her hand-held dictating machine, tapes, and
two fresh legal pads. She was humming as she sat down
to lock the lap drawer on her desk.

When her office door swung open, she almost gasped.
She hadn't expected anyone. Least of all Endor Thorogood.

"Judge Thoro—Endor. I—I didn't know you were still
here."

"Good evening, Darian. Don't get up. And you're
right, I'm not usually here past six, but there's something I need to talk to you about before morning. Something is going to come up at the staff meeting and you
need to be warned."

Warned? The look on his face frightened her. Judge
Thorogood liked her. Admired her work. He'd said so
within earshot of plenty of people, partners included. But
something was obviously wrong. His face was set like
granite, and the thin line around his lips told her he was
reining in his temper. In his right hand he had a set of
court papers. They were opened to a page where Darian
could see someone had made an angry red circle. Several
angry red circles.

He dropped the pleading on the desk in front of her.
"Read the answer to number eighty-one."

Darian scanned the paper, which was filled with answers to interrogatories. Questions propounded to them
by opposing counsel to try to discover all the facts and
circumstances of their case. She'd prepared the answers
herself and submitted them. Two, no three weeks ago.
She swallowed. Someone had circled one answer so hard,

the paper was torn. "'...reference page number eight in Dr. Albert Neuhaven's letter to...' Oh, my God. He's our expert."

Endor's face grew, if possible, slightly more glacial. "Precisely. I assume that, as any first-year law student would know, you realize this means you've opened the door to all the information Dr. Neuhaven has. They can now subpoena every bit of privileged and confidential material we've supplied to help him arrive at his findings. As well as any notes he's taken in private meetings with our client."

Darian was mute, her heart thumping in her chest. She felt as if a chasm had just yawned open at her feet. It was a stupid mistake. Careless. Sloppy. "I—I can't imagine how it got past me, Endor. I can't excuse my—my—"

He held up a hand, and his expression softened. Slightly. "You know, Darian, I've admired your work during your entire career at the firm. You've been one of our most outstanding associates ever, and I'd hate to see this blot your career." He rubbed his chin. "Now this doesn't have to be a disaster. Dr. Neuhaven's work, after all, is fairly minor in the scheme of the whole case."

He took a deep breath. "I've been thinking about this all afternoon, and I want to concentrate on damage control. For you and for us." He smiled a little, and a hint of his kindness flickered through his eyes. "You'll need to pull everything that we've given Neuhaven. And get copies of his bills to us and his time sheets. You have until tomorrow morning to figure out every possible angle where Neuhaven's information can damage us. You already have his files, I assume, since you're the one who prepared that." He prodded the offending paper lying on Darian's desk—its furious, concentric red circles still a throbbing accusation.

"I do. I think. No, I do, I'm sure."

"Good," he said, and stood. "I'll leave you to it, then." At the door, he glanced down and saw her things stacked and waiting. "Looks like I caught you just in time," he said. "Were you leaving?"

She looked up at him. "No," she said softly. "I'm not going anywhere."

Darian called and left a message on Tom's machine. When he called her, she told him what had happened, and he made sympathetic noises that she barely acknowledged.

Endor was right. The damage didn't have to be too bad as long as they could do some fast footwork before the other side noticed her glaring mistake. She berated herself mercilessly and prepared a memo exposing every possible way the other side could exploit her stupidity.

She worked until four-thirty that morning, took a cab to the Fallbrook and collapsed into bed for two hours.

The staff meeting was no less brutal than she deserved. Atwell glared at her and carved her up nicely in front of the other associates. Endor did not try to protect her, but let the full weight of her error fall squarely on her shoulders—exactly where it belonged. At the end of the meeting, though, he did compliment her work and say that he thought her recommendations for damage control were excellent, inspired even. She managed half a smile. No doubt the news of her error would be grinding merrily through the office rumor mill by lunchtime.

The rest of the day passed in a miserable blur. She executed her duties with military precision, though. Double-, even triple-checking every jot and title for the slightest error. As usual at three-thirty she called home and spoke with Jason and tried to sound cheerful. Tom was apparently working somewhere in Austin and left a message that he planned to spend the night in town with her.

He was waiting for her in the suite after work, and their dinner was quiet and strained. Tom was obviously trying to be polite and supportive, but knew there was nothing he could say. He'd already murmured as many encouraging, meaningless phrases as either of them could stand to hear. Even their lovemaking was awkward and out of sync.

Late that night, exhausted but unable to sleep, Darian lay propped up on one elbow, watching him. Tear after tear trailed unchecked out of her eyes. The shape of his shoulder was so beautiful, as was his strong muscular arm, and the ridges of his powerful torso. Everything hurt her. To love someone so much. To be held inside the arms yet outside the heart of someone she loved so much was an unbearable torture.

She thought of all the things she had wanted to say to him, and again felt despair welling up. *What's the use.* He didn't want her for that. How many times had he said how happy he was? How perfect his life had turned out to be? The coming baby thrilled him. She thought she felt a stirring in her center and touched her stomach.

This is what he wants. The capable, successful wife. The healthy, independent mother. She remembered Winnie the day of the auction flinging her body against her cage. Another tear slipped out, slid down her cheek and fell. No one was going to come rescue her, though.

She raised her fingers to his beautiful mouth, close enough to feel the sweet, warm rush of his breath, and felt her tears fall harder.

* * *

The next morning, alone in the shower, she cried again.

By the time Tom finished in the bathroom she was dressed, her briefcase waiting by the door, along with her leather bag and coat. He sat on the bed with a towel wrapped around his middle, humming and pulling on his socks.

"I was just thinking, honey," he said, "what do you think about naming her Caroline?" He gave her a quick smile over his shoulder. "If it should turn out to be a boy, I'd like to name him after my dad, but I don't care for the name Buford very much, do you? Of course, I really don't care one way or the other. I'll love little Buford or Caroline either way." He glanced up and gave her a quick smile. "Maybe it's twins—one of each. Wouldn't that be great?"

He talked on and on about trust funds and education, but Darian barely heard what he said. Every time they were alone, he talked about the baby. The awkwardness he'd felt the night before had obviously passed, and now he was once again ebullient and aglow with the prospect of impending fatherhood. Sitting there, half-naked on the bed, he radiated happiness and the apex of masculine power. Again, the sight of him pierced her. It was too much to bear. She couldn't face the pressure at the office, the baby growing inside her, and having him here and not loving her.

He belonged at the ranch, not here. She couldn't take it here. Not in a place that should be for lovers. She could be stronger at Clearpool, away from this pressure. But not here. "Tom."

"Hmm?"

"I was thinking . . ."

"Yes?"

He stood and pulled on his old-fashioned briefs, then his jeans. His belt buckle made a masculine, metallic clink with every button he fastened. He turned to face her, a pleasant expression resting easily on his handsome open features.

"I've been awfully tired here, you know. Working the long hours and all."

He stood still then. Alert. "Yes?" he said quietly.

"And I was thinking, maybe it would be best if we didn't try to spend time together here in town. I mean... I know the drive must tire you out, and you know—"

"I know exactly what you mean," he said. "If that's what you want, that's the way it'll be." He turned, sat back down on the bed, and began to pull on one of his boots. She crossed to him to kiss him but just as she reached him he leaned down, groping for the other boot under the bed.

She turned at the door and murmured goodbye, but apparently he didn't hear.

She didn't return to Clearpool for two more days. Dr. Neuhaven was called into the office and Darian, Richard, Atwell and Endor spent the better part of two afternoons helping him prepare truthful if unrevealing answers to any possible questions. Files and computers were purged, papers shredded and everything that could be taken care of without actually breaking a law was done. Several laws were bent until they squealed, and remarkably creative interpretations applied to some statutes, but every action remained within legal limits. Barely. When every possible measure had been taken, they settled down to see how long it would take the other side to notice Darian's mistake.

Darian found the old practice of "waiting for the other shoe to drop" to be emotionally and physically exhausting. Friday afternoon, Endor ordered her home and told her not to show her face in the office until the following Monday.

As she was packing her briefcase, he came in and sat down in one of her leather client chairs. "You know what Monday is, don't you?" he said with a sly smile.

Darian returned a smile of equal slyness. "Sure. The fourth."

His gray eyes narrowed, and a little smile edged up the corners of his mouth. "Is Tom in town much these days? Haven't seen much of him lately."

Darian kept her expression collected. "He's been really busy. I'm sure you've seen the dismal price of West Texas crude. And that banking thing hasn't done him much good, either."

"Why don't you invite him to meet with us for cocktails Monday afternoon? Here, in the partners' lounge."

In the partners' lounge?

Darian smiled. Grinned. "The *partners'* lounge?"

Endor reached out his hand. "Congratulations, and welcome to the firm. Of course the official announcement won't be until Monday, and so you mustn't tell anyone, but I know Tom will want to join us for our little celebration. About three o'clock, I think."

"Thank you, Endor. Judge Thorogood. I'm—I'm—"

"You're exhausted. Now go home to your husband and enjoy your weekend. Once you're a partner, you'll probably have to work harder. You always work hardest when you're working for yourself. Right?"

She smiled, a little wanly, she knew. "Right."

He paused at the door. "And, Darian. You know we start picking a jury in about nine months. Since the case is in federal court, we'll be down in Galveston, of course, and your partners were thinking it would be a good idea for you to do some of the preliminary demographics and jury research before our voir dire starts. Just a couple of weeks at a time, but you'll need to get started no later than August. No, don't thank me. Just something for you to think about. Well, have a nice weekend."

When the door thumped shut, Darian slowly lowered herself into her chair. She'd made partner. How many others at the firm would? Three. Four at the most.

"Well, my life just gets better every minute, doesn't it? I'm a full partner at Sternwell and Haig. Shoot up a flare."

Now go home to your husband and enjoy your weekend. Once you're a partner, you'll probably have to work harder. You always work hardest when you're working for yourself. Right?

Nausea bubbled in her stomach, and she slammed her briefcase closed. *Go here. Go there. Do this. Do that. Why do I have to do everything? Why can't I have feelings and be needy sometimes? The firm. Jason. Tom. Marty. Even the damn dog always wants something. Pet me. Feed me. Let me out. Let me in.*

Walking out of the office, she thought to herself, I'm sick of this. I'm a person, too. But do I get to complain? Do I get to have feelings? No. I have to be a mother and a lawyer and a wife. And a boss. And an employee.

When her tires shrieked in the parking lot, she realized she was pressing down too hard on the accelerator.

All the way out to Clearpool, she nursed her anger.
You're being unreasonable, she told herself. You're just
tired and upset. If you take this out on Jason and Tom
you'll feel guiltier. Take a deep breath. Relax.

By the time she pulled in next to Tom's truck, her head
was banging and her shoulders were too tight to even roll.
Winnie was outside, and when she saw Darian drive up,
she bounded forward, tongue lolling happily. As soon as
she got close enough to see into the truck, however, she
stopped in mid-bound, turned and trotted nervously back
to the porch, glancing fearfully over her shoulder as if she
expected to have a stick thrown at her. Darian narrowed
her eyes and jutted her jaw at the puppy.

As soon as she stepped into the house, she heard the
tinny roar of some television sporting event. The tightness in her shoulders ratcheted up a notch. She dropped
her purse and briefcase on the kitchen table. She never let
Jason put his things down where they served food, but
the act of defiance seemed justified. Even necessary.

Darian noticed a scrap of paper under the condiment
caddy. "*Darianita,* do you need anything from the market? Fresh produce is tomorrow, and I thought..."
Dominga's note asked if she wanted anything special
since Saturday was shopping day.

Darian stopped. Dominga was always thoughtful. Always patient. *Maybe I should wait a minute before I
storm in there like Sherman through Georgia. After all,
here's a nice weekend in front of us. I have good news. I
guess. I'll ask Dominga to get something special for dinner Saturday night. Something easy so I can cook.*

She opened her briefcase to take out a legal pad and
write Dominga a note. The only one she could find was

old, had hardly any pages left at all, and most of those had been scribbled on.

She flipped the pages over one at a time until she came to one marked up more than the others. There were darkened moisture rings on it where someone had set a glass down on it. No, two. There was a partial list on the paper. At the top, scrawled in her own happy, exaggerated penmanship were the words *Dearly Beloved.*

She traced the words with her fingers. She had been so happy that night as she had been writing her wedding plans. Intoxicated with happiness.

But she had not been dearly beloved. Had never been. Would never be.

She tore the bottom half of the paper off, wrote Dominga thanks, and told her, no, nothing special for that weekend. Then she walked through to see her son and husband.

Jason sat cross-legged on the floor, the remote control clutched in both hands, his head tipped back to look at the screen. He barely glanced up when she walked in.

"'Lo, Mom."

"Hi, honey. Good game?"

"Mmm."

"Where's Tom?"

"Don't know. He was here when you walked in, but he got up."

Darian felt her eyes narrow. *Don't lose your temper.* "I see."

She walked back to their bedroom, and when she opened the door, Tom barely glanced her way. He sat on the edge of the bed, talking on the phone. He wore jeans, but no belt and a plain white T-shirt. He was barefooted, and his strong feet rested squarely on the floor.

Darian felt an irrational flash of temper and shoved the door closed. Hard.

When it banged shut, Tom flinched and glared at her. "... finish this later, I'd appreciate it. Thanks, Ed." He dropped the phone into its cradle and leveled a hard look at her. "Welcome home."

"Thanks."

"What's the matter now?"

"Nothing, I was just thinking about your feet."

"My *feet?*"

"Yes."

"And that's why you slammed the door?"

"Well, I just don't think it's fair, do you? I mean, look at my shoes and look at yours. Women's shoes aren't even shaped like feet."

Tom's eyes widened and his head tipped to the side. He was speechless.

She leaned over and yanked off one of her two-hundred-dollar designer shoes. "Whose foot is shaped like this? Look at all my shoes. Look at all women's shoes. Pointy toes and stupid little straps and buckles and ... and look what they've done to my feet. Your feet aren't ruined. Men's shoes are shaped like men's feet. It's not fair."

He sat without moving. His eyes slid away. Then back. "What exactly happened at the office today?"

She hesitated. "I made partner."

"Oh, of course, I should have guessed. Congratulations. I can see how happy it's made you."

"Thank you."

She wanted to shout at him. But everything she thought of to say seemed stupid. *I have everything I ever wanted and I've changed my mind.* Or how about, *I know I promised one thing, but I've decided I don't want anything I said I wanted, and I do want the one thing I said I'd never endure. Is that okay with you? Would you like something special for dinner now?*

She just stood there, glaring, fists balled while an invisible vice closed around her chest.

He squeezed his eyes closed. Then he stood up slowly and folded his arms across his chest and rocked back slightly. When he looked at her again, his eyes were hard as agate and his lips pressed together in a straight, tough line.

"I can't stand living like this, Darian." He nodded down at the phone. "That was my lawyer. Monday morning, I'm invoking the separation provision in our prenuptial agreement. After the baby is born, I'm going to file for divorce."

Chapter Ten

Darian stood very still. Tom stared at her, his gaze hard and level. Outside, the tree clawed against the window, and dogs yammered in the distance.

"What?"

"You heard me," he said flatly. "I'm not living like this."

I'm invoking the separation provision in our prenuptial agreement. "But I'm . . . the baby—"

"Yes, I know, and I will take care of our children. That won't change, but I refuse to live this way." His eyes fell to her stomach, raked up to her face. "I apologize for the temporary inconvenience."

Darian felt the angry flush color her neck. *How dare he speak to me that way? He knows how I feel about this baby.* She glared at him. The line of vision seemed to crackle between them, ready to arc any moment in an angry discharge. Then the impact of his words began to settle in.

It's over. He's leaving.

Two more breaths. Three. How can I feel this way? she wondered. Her blood roared in her ears as if she were going to faint. The whole world stopped and left her enclosed in an island of perfect, silent misery.

His shoulders were squared, and his face was set with ugly determination. "I'm as much to blame as you, and I sure as hell regret my part in this. I didn't realize how stupid I was being. I thought that arranging this marriage on ideological and financial grounds was a real stroke of genius. I just knew a husband and wife could maturely plan a life together, share goals and what time they had. I wanted this so bad I convinced myself that this would be enough to make our life full." He stopped speaking for a moment and leveled his hardest gaze yet at her. "But nothing," he said, "nothing could be as empty as this marriage."

Darian felt his words thump into her like arrows. *Go ahead and say it. Tell me you don't love me and get it over with.* She tried to stay calm, although inside she was screaming like a woman fallen overboard. Her breath wheezed in and out of her body, and she felt the life inside her quiver. The internal trail of a tiny arm sweeping underneath her heart. She dropped her hand to feel, and her mouth opened slightly. "She's moving," she murmured.

Tom's eyes dropped to her stomach, and he grimaced as if he'd been knifed. "Don't do that to me," he said. "Haven't you done enough?"

Haven't you done enough?

That did it. "What do you mean, 'Haven't I done enough?' You're damn right, I've done enough. I've done everything a woman could do. More. I run around here like a lunatic trying to practice law and be a mother and a wife. I'm trying to do what everyone expects me to do, and I'm sick of it. I hate all of it and I don't want to do it anymore."

It was out. It didn't matter. He was leaving anyway, so she had nothing to lose.

"Well then, just what the hell *do* you want?"

His expression had changed, but she didn't bother to try to interpret it. She was sick of trying to be everything to everyone. She had nothing to lose. The one thing she wanted most was lost, and nothing else really mattered.

Well, maybe not quite. Some things would always matter. "You know, up to this instant I could have told you, but now I don't know exactly. I know I love this baby. I love my son. And I love you, Tom." Her voice cracked. She hated that. Another sign of her weakness.

"But I don't think I want my partnership. I'm sorry. I didn't mean for this to happen. It just... did." She couldn't look at him. Try to show a little dignity, she thought. "I know I've ruined everything, but I can't help it." She looked down. "I fell in love with you, and that changed everything."

Silence filled the room, and Darian was treated to several seconds of undiluted humiliation. She felt a little lighter, though. A little freer to be out from under the burden of deception.

"Well," he said quietly. "Was that so hard?"

She looked up. His eyes were bright, the blue turning aquamarine with emotion. "What?"

"Was that so hard to say?"

Her breath huffed out. "Well, actually, yes, it was."

He was moving across the room. Closer. His eyes had warmed. His expression softened. "I thought it might be. I didn't know if you were strong enough, but I had to take the chance. We'd never have made it if you hadn't been."

She folded her arms around herself, and stepped away from him. "Wait a minute. What is—what are you talking about?"

"What do you think? I love you, Darian. I've always loved you. From the minute you walked up to the tent, wearing those stupid green cowboy boots. I took one look and that was it for me."

"I don't understand. Why are you saying this now? You don't have to—"

"Oh, be quiet." He sighed. "You've been so busy trying to be strong and responsible—the ultimate professional. Be a good lawyer. Be a good mother. Be a good daughter. You wanted to be so perfect, you weren't being very human. You wouldn't reach out." He smiled, but he didn't look very happy. "If you wouldn't reach out to me, how could you love me?"

She looked up at him suspiciously. "Why didn't you tell me, then? It would have been a lot easier."

"No, it wouldn't. You would never have admitted to yourself that you loved me until you were forced to. In the first place, you didn't want to love me. And then admitting it would mean turning your back on everything that got you by for so long." He shrugged. "I wasn't sure if you'd ever admit to yourself that you loved me. Much less admit it to me."

He sighed. "And after that last day we spent at the Fallbrook..." His voice revealed hurt and betrayal Darian never knew he felt. Things he'd hidden from her filled his eyes. Accusation. Pain. His own humiliation. "You told me not to come back. Do you know how that makes a man feel? Especially after what had happened between us? I thought—"

"But I was afraid you didn't love me. I thought you just came to the hotel to be a...a good guy, you know. Supportive and all that. But I wanted more. I wanted to be..."

"What?"

She looked up at him and shrugged. "It's stupid."

"Tell me. Say it."

"Beloved. Like in the wedding. I want to be your dearly beloved."

"But you are."

He opened his arms, inviting her in.

Did he really say it? Is this real?

The look on his face told her it was. More than admiration and affection radiated from it. She saw love in his eyes, real love. The same kind of powerful emotion she knew he must have felt from her. She moved forward one step. Two. Stepped into powerful arms that closed possessively around her. "Why did you marry me? I mean really?" she asked.

"Because I loved you."

"Then all that stuff you said back then and again today about similar goals and life outlook—"

"Bull— Uh, hogwash. I'd have said anything. Done anything. I suppose I started planning this from the start, from the first day. I'm sure glad Jason decided to—"

His words ended abruptly, and Darian looked up. His brow was furrowed.

"What?"

"I shouldn't say," he said. "It's betraying a confidence."

"What are you talking about?"

He looked down at her. "I'll do this once, but never again. Jason never said anything about it to me until afterward, but that business with that big kid—"

"Tykie Wilguneski?"

"Yeah. It was a setup deal."

"A what?"

"He paid Tykie to say that stuff, but it was all lies. He was trying to get expelled from Fullingham."

"But why? He loved that school."

"He was worried sick about you. He was afraid you were working yourself to death to send him there, and that you'd die and leave him."

"Oh, my God. Why would he think that?"

Tom shrugged. "He worries about you. He also said that since he was the man in the family, you were his responsibility. You know what his exact words were? He said, 'The one who has the power is the one who has the responsibility.' That's some sentiment, isn't it, coming from a ten-year-old? He thought since he had the power to change things, it was his job."

"Oh, no." Darian looked away miserably. "I know I've said that, but I never meant that to apply to him. Not a little boy. He never said anything to me."

"No, but he did to me." He chuckled. "You know what he said? He said he could relax because you were my responsibility now."

"Tom, I never meant to pass that on to him, but you see, somewhere inside me there's a person who grew up thinking she was undeserving and inadequate, and so I fought that. I used all my talents and what brains I had to prove that wasn't true. Then for years that's the way I thought of myself. Smart, competent, professional me. I was proving to the world that I deserved recognition and respect because I earned it—"

"I know all that. And you did earn it, sweetheart. You're a hell of lawyer—"

"Yes, but that's not why I deserve it. I deserve respect because I'm a decent person. I don't have to be some kind of dancing bear and perform for rewards—"

"Well, I know that. Who doesn't?"

"Me. I didn't. And then when I realized I wanted to quit my job, I thought it proved that I deserved to be abandoned. That I was a quitter. You know, no good."

He closed his arms more tightly and she clutched at him, still speaking against his shirt. Against the sweet smell of his clothes and the ghost of the old-fashioned after-shave he'd used sometime that morning. "And you know what? I do want to quit, Tom. I'm tired of all this, and I don't want to do it anymore. My life means different things now. Sometimes I think I just want to be out at Clearpool with you and Jason and our baby. But then I get worried again. I'm not sure I'll be able to do that. I mean, I know I'm supposed to use my abilities and all. What if . . ."

Despite Tom's tenderness toward her, despair welled up again, gnawing at her with familiar accusations. "You see? I *am* just as bad as Joel. How will anyone be able to live with me? How will I live with myself? But I don't want to work fifteen hours a day for—"

"Hush," he said, and tilted her head back to look into her eyes. His hands were on both sides of her face, forcing her to look up at him. "There's another answer, you know."

"What?" She was ashamed of the desolation in her voice—what a pathetic way for a grown woman to carry on.

He stroked her face, pushing back her hair with gentle fingers. "In case you haven't noticed, Steinbuck Enterprises could use a little help."

"What?"

"You know, you say that a lot."

"*Tom.*"

"I realize oil and gas isn't your field, but you're fairly bright. With hard work and a little more attention to detail, you can probably—ow." He laughed. "I deserved that."

"Yes, you did."

"I don't know how you feel about working in a family business, but the benefits are good." He ran his thumb lightly over her mouth, kissed her. "And our maternity-leave policy is great. Take as many years off as you like. And come back whenever you're ready. Full partnership guaranteed."

His left hand dropped to her stomach. "This may happen more than once, you know."

"Oh, I hope so," she said, and wound her arms around his neck. Still, there was something she had to know. Had to ask. "Tom, how far were you willing to go? I mean, would you really have invoked the separation provision in the... Wait a minute, there's no separation provision in our prenuptial."

He snorted with laughter. "I know. I was afraid you'd remember that."

He pulled her closer, smoothed back her hair and kissed her temple, her forehead. "No, love," he murmured. "There is no separation provision. None necessary. I will never let you go. And I know you love me too much to leave me. I *always* knew it."

She wanted to punch him. Or kiss him. "But why? Why did you say such a thing? It was mean."

"I was bluffing. You know, like in a card game."

"I never play cards."

He grinned. "I know."

She looked up at him. "Say it again."

"My dearly beloved," he said quietly. "I'll be telling you I love you every day and every night for the rest of our lives."

* * * * *

Get Ready to be Swept Away by
Silhouette's Spring Collection

Abduction
& Seduction

These passion-filled stories explore both the dangerous
desires of men and the seductive powers of women.
Written by three of our most celebrated authors, they are
sure to capture your hearts.

Diana Palmer
Brings us a spin-off of her Long, Tall Texans series

Joan Johnston
Crafts a beguiling Western romance

Rebecca Brandewyne
New York Times bestselling author
makes a smashing contemporary debut

Available in March at your favorite retail outlet.

MILLION DOLLAR SWEEPSTAKES (III)

is
DIANA PALMER'S
THAT BURKE MAN

He's rugged, lean and determined. He's a
Long, Tall Texan. His name is Burke, and he's
March's *Man of the Month*—Silhouette Desire's
75th!

Meet this sexy cowboy in Diana Palmer's
THAT BURKE MAN, available in March 1995!

Man of the Month...only from Silhouette Desire!

 **Silhouette ROMANCE**™

BELIEVING IN MIRACLES
by
Linda Varner

Carpenter Andy Fulbright and Honorine "Honey" Truman had all the criteria for a perfect marriage—they liked and respected each other, they desired and needed each other...and *neither* one loved the other! But with the help of some mistletoe and two young elves, these two might learn to believe in the miracle of Christmas....

BELIEVING IN MIRACLES is the second book in Linda Varner's MR. RIGHT, INC., a heartwarming series about three hardworking bachelors in the building trade who find love at first sight— construction site, that is!

Don't miss BELIEVING IN MIRACLES, available in December. And look for Book 3, WIFE MOST UNLIKELY, in March 1995. Read along as old friends make the difficult transition to lovers....

Only from **Silhouette**®

where passion lives.